Since We Last Spoke

Also by Brenda Rufener

Where I Live

Since We Last Spoke

BRENDA RUFENER

An Imprint of HarperCollinsPublishers

HarperTeen is an imprint of HarperCollins Publishers.

Since We Last Spoke
Copyright © 2019 by Brenda Rufener
All rights reserved. Printed in the United States of America.
No part of this book may be used or reproduced in any manner whatsoever
without written permission except in the case of brief quotations embodied in
critical articles and reviews. For information address HarperCollins Children's
Books, a division of HarperCollins Publishers,
195 Broadway, New York, NY 10007.
www.epicreads.com

ISBN 978-0-06-257108-3

19 20 21 22 23 PC/LSCH 10 9 8 7 6 5 4 3 2 1

First Edition

For Bryan

I imagine one of the reasons people cling to their hates so stubbornly is because they sense, once hate is gone, they will be forced to deal with pain.

—James A. Baldwin

Since We Last Spoke

1

Aggi

MY SISTER KATE TOLD ME love was glue, a strong adhesive holding people together. She swore it worked as a protective layer of bulletproof glass, something shatter-free. *Love sticks together when the world around you fractures into pieces*, Kate said. But if unprotected, love will shatter, too.

When I wish for one more moment with my sister, sitting on the moss-covered dock, swinging our legs in unison, while we skip rocks across the glassy lake water, these thoughts overwhelm me. I want to ask Kate what protective force she was talking about, because love has only shown me how fragile and frail it is, even in the strongest relationships that take a lifetime, or in my case, seventeen years, to create.

Six thousand two hundred and five days for me to fall in love with Maxwell Granger and seconds for our relationship to smash apart. The glue Kate referenced didn't stick, and I'm not sure a strong enough adhesive exists to hold together what was ripped from Max and me.

If only Kate received texts, I could ask what she meant. But my sister will never see the hundreds of messages I keep sending to her number. Cell service won't reach her.

An engine rumbles in the distance, growing louder as the gears grind and rip the packed and unpacked snow. After a fresh blanket unfolds over Walabash Woods, noise softens, but as soon as a vehicle rounds the turn onto the mile-long private road that leads to the driveway my family shares with Max and his parents, the engine purr becomes a roar, and my movements follow the crescendo. Snow has a way of controlling me—slowing me down, or speeding me up—but today is Friday, and as on most Fridays, I'm determined to conquer its hold.

I stomp the mat where *Welcome to the Frank Home* has worn, smudged by ice and shoes, and kick my boots from my feet in midrun as I race for the stairs. Each step moans and creaks, and when I hit the top landing the banister rumbles, on the verge of collapse. I dodge an open box of nails layered in dust and leap over a stack of Sheetrock piled in the hall on the way to my room. Strangers might think we're in the middle of a remodel, which is true if "the middle" means purgatory. I do wish one of those people from HGTV would pop their head in the door and shout, *Surprise!* or *Welcome home, Frank family!* or at the very least, *Get the hell out while we gut this farmhouse and make it livable again!* Then I wouldn't have to wonder how many months the same box of nails will sit untouched in the middle of the hall outside my room, like a dirty sock in the street everyone circles around to avoid. Anything designed to improve life stopped after the accident. My life, my family crumbled with the Sheetrock.

Last December, though, I was standing naked in a canoe off the shore of Plum Lake, shouting, "Maxwell Granger, I love you more than you love yourself!" My arms outstretched, chin aimed at the clouds that were spitting white dots into my hair like tiny balls of paper.

It had taken years to finally show Max what my heart had kept concealed since we were kids. The whole naked part? I'd lost a bet among my closest friends but embraced it as a win. Nothing was going to stop my confession—not even losing a foot race to the dock that sent me into my family's canoe, unclothed and unafraid. I placed the bet on purpose, and I lost on purpose, too. I knew exactly what I wanted to do that day. It felt like my life's mission.

Umé, wrapped in smiles and all the confidence of the universe, screamed from the shore, "Jesus George Clooney Christ, Aggi! Your ass will be ice. And where is your damn life jacket? How many times have I insisted you don't climb into a canoe without . . ."

Umé, my best friend since middle school, also known as my life anchor. We met in gym class as the kids were lining up, ready to count off by twos and split into teams. Hands clamped onto my shoulders and a head popped beside my ear. A voice whispered, "I'm going to steer you to the bathroom. Don't worry, I'm right behind you. Just keep your feet together—shuffle—and don't look down at your legs."

But it was too late. Two streams of blood trickled down my bare inner thighs.

Umé, thankfully quick with a little white lie, shouted to our PE teacher, "She's going to be sick!" and guided me into the restroom stall before our teacher protested or anyone saw that I'd started my period at the most inopportune time. Umé's warm hand on my back has pulled, and sometimes pushed, me through the bad days, horrible times, and moments of complete devastation. Someday, I wish to return the favor.

Max's best friend, Henry, wrapped in toilet paper from the waist down, as he'd lost a similar bet, hollered from the dock, "What'd I tell you, Max? She loves you! Always has, you lucky sumbitch!"

Henry didn't mean Max was lucky because *I* loved him. He meant love in the more general sense. You see, Henry needs love like he needs air, but he miraculously grows, and even thrives, without it. Henry's like this giant beanstalk that shoots toward the stars even though he's never watered or fed or told how much he's loved and appreciated at home. Henry's found a place to store love, pack it away somewhere deep inside him. Then he lavishes his friends with it, especially Max. Who's the lucky sumbitch now?

Since elementary school, Henry and Max have been

friends, though Max has never stepped foot inside Henry's camp trailer. None of us have. Henry won't allow his friends near his home hidden away in the woods, and not because he's ashamed or embarrassed, though I'm sure that plays a part, but because Henry wants to keep his friends safe. When we hike Walabash Woods, none of us go within a quarter mile of Henry's chained-off driveway. Any closer and the dogs, Henry's father, and his twin brothers would bark at us to keep off their private property. My dad says the Beacons have a lively record with the law and don't want anyone close to their property. All the rules in the world, though, couldn't keep Henry from his friends, especially Max. Those two have become like brothers.

That day at the lake, Max kicked at the snow-packed shore, his laughs bounding off tree to tree, wrapping my words in a warm blanket. Bravery never came easy for me. I dared not share the secrets in my heart until that day, minute, second. A ridiculous game of truth or dare among friends that suddenly became all dare. But when I threw my head back and laughed from the deepest parts of my gut, I grew so sure of many things. Myself. Max. Our future together.

Max cupped his hands around his mouth. "You're naked! In the lake! In the middle of a snowstorm! Aggi Frank, you're as wild as Walabash Woods!"

"Wildly in love with you!" I shouted.

Max tore his hat from his head and threw it at the lake. A decision he'd later regret when his ears practically froze off his face as he carried me back to my clothes, neatly folded beside the bonfire he'd built behind our families' communal barn. For the record, I was still naked during Max's deliberate act of chivalry, but quickly scrambled for my clothes. Max said he was protecting me from frostbitten feet. But I had willingly dumped my self-reliance into the snow and demanded a lift. In that moment, I knew I'd climb Everest without shoes if at journey's end Max were there with wide arms and hands bearing mugs full of hot cocoa. While love oozes from somewhere deep inside Henry, comfort percolates from Max. Well, it used to, anyway.

The woods ushered in my love-filled confession to Max with ease. Snowflakes fell and stacked like Jenga blocks made of marshmallows. The gaps between snowflakes cushioned our background noise until the woods fell silent, still. Then my arms reached east to west and the sky unfolded a thick blanket of snow that covered my naked body. The lake hushed and the silence gave me courage to tell Max how I'd felt for longer than I remembered.

The woods had known Max and me since we were weaving in and out of our mothers' legs, tumbling over while we reached for the same pinecone or teased at a squirrel tail. Walabash Woods knew I'd never tell Max how I felt until the time was right. After the flakes began to fall. Before the ice on the water cracked and split in two.

My words were snowflakes, floating in the sky, never sharing what they'd gone through before tumbling to earth. When you stick out your tongue and the ice crystals melt, you don't feel the billions of water molecules that fought to stay intact while temperatures shifted and changed. You don't taste how the winds banged against the kernels of ice as they plunged through layers of air and broke into pieces. Snowflakes only share their beauty when their journey ends. You only see the artful design after they land. Snowflakes never reveal the hell it took to form them.

Last winter on the lake, when I told Max I loved him, the woods applauded my courage with chirps and hoots. Pine branches bowed, and lake water applauded by splashing against the rocks. Even a damn loon—rare in western North Carolina—burst into laughter as it flew overhead. Possibilities had no end for me and Max, only beginnings. We were at the start of something magical, something meaningful, something supposed to last forever. In that moment, we felt our love was endless and shatter-free.

That night, Max's brother was killed in a car accident. Ten days later, my sister Kate died by suicide.

These events changed everything. These events destroyed us.

I jab a mechanical pencil between the slats of my bedroom blinds and peek across the snow-packed figure-eight tracks connecting my driveway to Max's. Pine trees, cloaked in white armor, line our property and stand guard. Sunlight bounces off the snowbanks and shoots against the wall mirror behind me, warming a small spot on my back. The thermostat is set to fifty-five degrees, so I shift in my chair hoping the sun spot will somehow increase my body temperature. Dad says, or rather shouts, that "heat costs money" and unless I "own stock in the electric company, the temperature stays at fifty." Dad probably wishes he owned stock. Mom wishes we had money. I just wish Dad had a job so he could make money.

Mom and I aren't supposed to know Dad lost both of his jobs months ago for smashing Max's father's face into the hood of his work truck. Mom and I aren't supposed to question why Dad leaves every morning dressed in Dickies and work boots, his shirt wrinkled and untucked. Mom glances out the window when Dad stomps through the kitchen on his way to not-work, never questioning, as if she refuses to confront what has happened. But I do, and when the opportunity presents itself, Dad's secret's going to blow up in his face. I just hope Mom's not staring out the window when it happens so she'll finally acknowledge the truth. Maybe even do something about it.

At 3:59 on a Friday, I sit at my desk, waiting for Max to plow his Jeep across the driveway. He'll arrive in sixty seconds. Hop into the snow and race for the passenger-side door. I wonder who the girl will be this week. I wonder if she will be someone I know, a lake kid, or a girl from town.

The engine hums louder, and I slide off my chair and crouch next to my desk at the window. Within seconds, Max plows into the driveway and slams the Jeep into park. I squint, but the girl's face is only a smudge of pink against the white canvas. She's not the same girl Max brought home last week, or the week before. This one's fluffier, brighter, and wearing a smile that would make strangers notice and nod. She's wrapped in a Chantilly cream–colored coat and a to-die-for azure-blue scarf. I'd definitely wear that scarf.

Max reaches for the girl's hand and she dips her toe into the snow and laughs. Pom-poms on her boots skid along the drifted powder and trail her footprints. Max motions for her to stay at his Jeep before racing toward his house to snatch a snow shovel from the porch. He clears a path to his front step and nods when he's finished. I half expect Max to throw down his coat, spin around, and magically unveil a checked flannel, wood axe, and earflap hat. Max, a gentleman and a lumberjack. At least the Max I remember.

Max stares at his feet as the girl sweeps her hair to one side and crunches snow on her way to the porch. I hate watching, but I can't seem to stop torturing myself. As many times as I've tried distracting myself after school, joining Umé for coffee or sitting on my bed with earbuds stuffed in my ears, I watch the clock to make sure I'm crouched beneath my win dow at this time every Friday.

Max rips off his hat and sinks his fingers deep into his night-colored hair. I shut my eyes and sigh, as the Jeep door opens. Max, now rubbing the back of his neck, pats powdered flakes off his pants, reaches inside the vehicle, and grabs his backpack from the floorboard and a pizza box from the dash.

9

My stomach growls, and I imagine the piping-hot, mouth-watering contents of that cardboard box. A Lucio & Sons large BLT, though Max hates both the L and the T.

For years I suggested to Max he keep it simple and order a bacon pizza, but this is Max we're talking about. In line, a couple of summers ago, I suggested Max ask Lucio & Sons' pizza person to please remove ingredients one is disgusted by, but Max, famous for complicating the simplest of shit, refused, and will therefore always scrape off lettuce and tomato from his bacon-lettuce-tomato pizza. He said he *wouldn't, couldn't, mess up a work of art: Lucio & Sons Picasso Pizza Pies.*

Max pushes the Jeep door shut with his hip. The girl on the porch stomps snow from her boots, then pauses to watch Max hesitate at the bottom step. He's back to staring at the ground, packing snow into V shapes with his feet. Max turns from the wraparound porch and scans the crescent-shaped lake in front of our property. He cranes his neck to the right, as he does every Friday just after four o'clock, until his eyes land on my house. He lifts his chin in slow motion and targets the window above my garage. My bedroom.

Max knows I'm here, peeking through the blinds, perched in my wooden chair, attempting to predict when the next ice storm will hit. This is my new hobby and my new life since the accident. I spend a lot of time analyzing wave motions in the atmosphere, trying to bring peace and order to weather-related chaos. Maybe Max understands part of what I do, but he doesn't see the whole picture.

For months, Max has lived my afternoon routine, as I sit in my dark, cold room, sneaking glances across the driveway. So much has changed since Kate. Since Max's brother, Cal. Since the tragedy that tore our families apart.

I've become keenly aware of Max's moves, too. How he's taken up running. How he's consuming a lot of pizza for his wiry frame. And how he brings a different girl home every Friday afternoon when he has the house to himself.

Max pauses and stares at my window for ten seconds. I count, as I always do, and hold my breath.

Max drops his chin. I clutch my chest.

What will you do this time, Maxwell Granger? I have the house to myself, too.

He shifts his weight and I flinch. Today could be the day. Am I ready? Max turns toward the porch and I raise my blind.

My sudden movement causes Max to whip back around and glance at my window. I stuff my hand into my front pocket to prevent it from doing something lawless, like waving.

Max's eyes lock onto my sweatshirted silhouette. No smile. No wave. No motioning for me to join him in the driveway.

What now Max? Whose move is it, anyway?

My heart drums as it does when I swim across the lake.

Talking to Max would violate the order. Break my dad's rule. *You will never speak to that boy again.*

I stand still and wait.

Why do you watch me, Max? Why do you still pretend to care?

11

Seconds pass the halfway mark, and my chest pinches with fear that Max is about to do something we'll both regret, so I beat him to the punch, drop my blinds, and they slam against the sill, rattle the window, chip off flakes of peeling paint. Max's eyes pierce mine while I twist the wand tight to shut him out of my sight. My back slides down the wall until my butt hits the floor.

I won't cry. The tears stopped months ago. Instead, I crouch beneath my window and wait for snow to crunch, laughs to echo from the porch.

Keys jingle. Max's dog barks. His words bellow and sink my heart before they are swallowed up by the snowbanks.

"We have the house to ourselves!" he says, though it sounds like a shout.

I peek through a thin gap in the blind as Max stares back at my house.

"Yeah. I heard you, Maxwell Granger," I whisper.

The slam of the front door sends sound waves skating across the snow from his house and crashing into mine.

2

MAX

I KICK THE FRONT DOOR closed and rush my basset hound, Pawtrick Swayze, into the kitchen before he jumps on the girl I've regretfully invited into my living room. He barks and snarls, and I squeeze his tube-shaped torso like a football and send him packing into his crate beside the pantry.

I wander the kitchen in circles, trying to gather my thoughts and compose myself, as I slip off my coat and toss it on a bar stool. I forgot to take the girl's coat. That's what a guy like Ryan Gosling would do. But I'm flustered, and besides, the coat rack sits right beside the front door. She's bound to see it. I draw a deep breath, swirl my temples. Pawtrick barks, and I jump. Seeing Aggi in the window makes me feel like there's something I should do, if only I knew what that *something* was.

"Thought you wanted pizza?" the girl shouts from the living room, and I collapse onto the counter.

Why do I keep doing this to myself? I mean, I know *why*. My symptom. A problem? *No*. The therapist definitely referred to it as a symptom, like loss of appetite, but every time I try to test myself in this area, see if the symptom no longer exists, I'm filled with remorse. I exhale, push myself off the counter, and shake my arms and roll my neck as my skin tingles and thaws in the warm kitchen.

I should never have invited her here. It's unfair to her and I need time to think. When I'm alone, though, my thoughts visit unwanted places, so here I am, standing in the kitchen beside my dog's crate while there's a wonderful human being sitting on my couch with a Lucio & Sons large BLT pizza. And Aggi. She's only feet from me, shutting her stupid blinds in her stupid room, probably wishing she'd never met stupid me.

My dog yelps, and I squat at his cage, letting him lick my fingers. "Exactly, Pawtrick. Exactly how I feel." Caged and restrained.

"I'm going to start eating without you!" the girl calls. The girl. Britney? Leslie? Lynn? I can't remember her name, because I am an asshole and have none of my shit together.

On the couch, BritneyLeslieLynn swings a piece of pizza in my direction. "You're the one who wanted to stop and get something to eat. Aren't you hungry?"

The vertex angle of her slice folds and flops as she waves it in the air. I feel like she's sending me a message, but I know it's in my head, as I've told no one about my problem—I mean, symptom. However, I nod at the commonality between the limp crust and me.

I sit on the couch beside her, and she chucks a couple of bacon chunks into her mouth. I smile, as does she. But I'm smiling at memories, not at the present situation. She reminds me of Aggi. Comfortable, confident.

"So when do your parents get home?"

I chuckle. She's forthright, too. So Aggi.

"Not for a while." I scoot back on the couch and pet the armrest like it's my dog.

"You look nervous."

My back straightens. "Do I? I do? I don't feel nervous." Complete lie.

She laughs and takes another bite of pizza.

If I had game, and if that's what those with game even call it, I'd make a move. This is where I'm supposed to reach over and ask if I can touch her. No. That sounds ridiculous. Not the asking but the touching. Guys do this shit, though, with girls they take home. Girls sitting on their couch asking when their parents will arrive. Guys un-Max-like, that is. I do things like sketch shapes on my jeans, forget to make eye contact, pet the couch like it's Pawtrick Swayze, and think about the girl I wish were here. The one who laughs only when I really deserve it. The one who can out-eat me in pizza. The one who's lived next door to me since we were babies.

She scrunches her napkin into a ball and drops it onto the coffee table, stands, takes my hand, and nods toward the stairs.

Okay, I think. *I can do this.* I slide to the edge of my couch and brake without delay. My hand slips from her grip. *I can't do this. Not today. Probably not ever.*

Ryan Gosling does this shit in every Ryan Gosling movie. He hops to his feet, rips off his shirt, pounds his hairless chest. Girls—women—seem to eat it up. I am not Ryan Gosling. I am not even close.

"Are you coming?" she asks. "If we're going to do this, shouldn't we get started?"

I nod with no intention of moving from the couch. Now I have to figure out how to ask her to leave, which is going to be difficult since I'm the one who invited her here.

"Well?"

I look up from my feet and shrug.

"Oh, God."

"I'm sorry. I'm incredibly sorry. It's just that—"

She whips around and snatches her purse from the side table. "Not sure why I thought you were better. Wasn't therapy supposed to cure you?"

Cure? I wish. Besides, I haven't seen a counselor in months. It's not exactly the kind of place I want to get in touch with my feelings, when Mom and Dad sit like statues next to me on the couch while I try to figure out the right words for *I haven't been able to get an erection in months. I need to know if this is part of the grieving process.*

16

"What do you know about my therapy, anyway?" I stuff both hands in the front pockets of my jeans.

She ties her scarf into a complicated knot. "Jess said, Katherine said, Lei Lei said."

I scoff. "Of course they did."

"You should just take me home."

I step into my boots. "You know, you shouldn't believe everything you hear about me."

I'm still not sure exactly what she's heard, but word travels fast at school, so I can only imagine.

"Okay, Max," she says flatly and zips her coat. "Just take me home, or should I call someone? Aggi, maybe?"

I wince. "Why Aggi?"

Her eyebrow lifts and she sighs. This is an effect I have on people. Acquaintances, even friends. When I insist I'm okay, people sigh. It lets them off the hook. They feel as though they can move on from an otherwise uncomfortable conversation. My therapist sighs, but I don't think it's out of exhaustion or annoyance or even relief. I think she sighs because I won't open up. But what do I know?

"I really am sorry," I say as I open the door.

She stops on the porch. "I know, and that's what makes this so sad." She glances over at Aggi's house, then back at me. "I really feel sorry for you. What you've gone through. What your families are dealing with. This shit's tough."

I'm grateful there's no sarcasm in her tone, but she turns abruptly and stomps down the steps. I suppose I deserve the cold shoulder. I invited her to my house for selfish reasons. I knew I'd see Aggi in the window. Her silhouette greets me nearly every day. Aggi, in that oversized sweatshirt, hair pulled up into a messy bun that draws her cheeks into sharp points. She's every time period of art mixed into one master-piece. Sharp edges in one spot, rounded corners in another. Eyes I can't figure out. Do they belong in the Medieval or Pre-Raphaelite period?

I grab the back of my neck and squeeze. A grin forces its way out. It's incredibly difficult not to laugh at the mess I've become, at the actual shit that is now my life.

3

Aggi

AS ON EVERY NIGHT SINCE the accident, dinner plans belong to me. My little sister, Grace, lives with Mom's boss and only remaining friend, Dr. Nelson, five to six nights a week. A light bulb went off in my mother's brain after Kate's death. Mom said she needed time to process grief, and who can think with a ten-year-old on your lap begging for kisses and hugs after her big sister died? I suggested I stay with Dr. Nelson, too, because Grace and I need each other, but Dad said, "Hell no!" and when Dad says, "Hell no!" he means he wants control and is afraid who I will run to if I'm not being controlled. So I stay home, make dinner for myself, and eat alone.

At the refrigerator, I rummage for packages of food that have not passed their expiration date. There is no sense waiting for the oven or stovetop to heat with Grace gone, so I prepare cold foods for myself. A bowl of cereal. A sandwich. A spoonful of peanut butter.

After Cal died and Kate was still in the hospital, I grilled fluffernutter sandwiches, Grace's favorite, stuffed them into Dad's old lunch box, clutched Grace's arm, and headed for the lake. Grace in her puffy coat and gloves, me in my down-filled parka. We'd sit on the dock, shivering, but warm on the inside as we had each other and we were still together. My heart broke for Max and his family, but I believed time would heal our families and we'd get through the loss if I focused on the one person my parents put me in charge of: Grace.

But one evening, Dad returned from the hospital to check on us and Max's father met him in our driveway. Shouts first. Then fists. Blows.

Dad caught a glimpse of us on the porch, spoke to me with his eyes, and I knew to rush Grace away from the house and down to the lake. Max followed us to the dock, but his father's pain froze his steps. Mr. Granger's heart fractured and broke so loudly the woods stopped moving, including Max. The heartbreak he felt over losing his brother surfaced, too, and slowed his stride, pushed at his spine until he couldn't lift his head. All while his father shouted, "Kate did this! If she hadn't gone! If she hadn't driven! If she . . . If she . . . If she . . ." Max never made it to the dock where we were sitting. He paced the trail, wandered in circles, then disappeared into the trees.

Paperwork now prevents our fathers from coming to blows but hasn't stopped the blame.

Before mom sent Grace to live with Dr. Nelson, I'd bundle my sister in her coat and we'd run to the dock. We both needed to be there. Alone but together. The sandwiches tasted better when we were sitting outside watching snowflakes drop and dance before hitting the lake. I wish Grace were here now so we could dangle our legs while we tore at the crust and smacked our lips when the marshmallow fluff froze on our mouths. The snowstorms outside my house don't hold a candle to the storm that brews on the inside.

A casserole dish with a brick of lasagna looks appetizing but reminds me of Kate. Two weeks after she died, casseroles brought into our home by local Plum Lake residents emptied and the dishes stacked in the sink. I decided to make dinner for my family. I thought if we sat together at the table and talked about how much we missed Kate, we'd draw closer. I'd read a grief article online that suggested Grace, the youngest and most vulnerable family member, needed to see us together. And I did, too. I wanted to talk to Mom and Dad about Kate. I wanted to remember funny things she said. I needed us to cry together. Empty dams had already begun to build between us. But the article said tears would connect us. Lasagna, I believed, would hold us together as love was supposed to do.

After I spent hours in the kitchen preparing homemade pasta and spreading it with oily sauce, Mom sent Grace to Dr. Nelson's, then disappeared behind her bedroom door. I waited up for Dad, though. He'd want to sit and talk at the

21

table as we used to. He'd fork the noodles and comment on their texture. He'd thank me and tell me to save him another plate for breakfast, and I'd save one for Mom, too. When our stomachs were full, he'd build a fire and ask me to stay up with him while we talked about Kate and what a great singer she was. How the song lyrics Kate wrote sounded so beautiful when Cal put her words to music. We'd remember how Kate could outswim anyone at Plum Lake, and I'd share how she was the best big sister and friend anyone could dream of having. But I was naive.

When Dad stumbled into the house after midnight, I zipped into the kitchen and popped his plate into the microwave, then watched as he stumbled to the counter, peeled back an aluminum lid from a can of Cirrus's cat food, and spread the meat onto a slice of bread with his finger. He folded the bread in half and bit the center. Not even a wince.

I said, "Hey, Dad. That's cat food you're eating."

He yanked the plate of lasagna from my hands and smashed it against the wall. Dad doesn't remember that moment in the kitchen, or if he does, he won't mention it, but the tomato sauce soaked into the flat eggshell paint and the wall turned pastel pink. The stain reminds me Dad has changed. He's angry, but for all the wrong reasons. Now, every time I walk into the kitchen and see the salmon stain on the wall, I remember how much my family has changed. And I grow angry, too.

But to protect myself, I have established boundaries. Like Mom's idea to send Grace away. Like Dad's enforcement of the law. His rule. I now live by a three-ingredient rule.

When I'm outside my room longer than it takes to sling together three ingredients, the air thickens and becomes stagnant. My chest tightens. Outdoors, in school, or even in my bedroom with the door closed, my chest moves without labor, but this house reminds me of losing everyone I love, and the pressure of loss is like a weight on my chest, crushing and flattening who I once was.

Grace goes to Dr. Nelson's, and the only one left to care for at home is Cirrus the cat. But even as I feed Cirrus, the house and all its memories squeeze my neck. Grace has felt the pressure, too. In the tiny window of time Grace is allowed to be at home, her eyes hollow and her spirit shrivels. It's the house, I know it, and it's strangling her. No matter how hard it is to live here without Grace, I'm glad she's gone. At least when Grace is with Dr. Nelson, I know she's not ignored. My little sister won't hear the hurtful words that will prick her heart and leave holes that will stick with her as she ages. It's better that I'm the pincushion.

My mouth dries, throat pinches. I've been out of my safe space for too long. Every room in this dilapidated house reminds me of Kate. Space she consumed, pictures she posed for, furniture she touched. Even when Cirrus, the cat our parents gave us for Christmas right before Kate died, purrs and rubs her white fur against my shins, my chest aches.

I stomp the hardwood, and Cirrus dives beneath the table and licks her paw. The cat is as much to blame as the rest of us. Even her purrs and fur couldn't comfort Kate and give her the lifeline she needed to stay alive and with us.

This is what happens when I'm out of my room for too long. I point fingers of blame, too. But the cat? All the anger and hate and blame that have absorbed into the walls rub off on me. My tolerance level is low after seeing Max with someone new, the pizza we should be devouring together, and that fresh snow that we used to play in, as it fell like torn cotton balls. I spin around, spiraling a strand of hair around my finger. My stamina is dangerously low today. I snatch two ingredients from the top shelf of the fridge and race upstairs toward my room.

When I kick the door shut behind me, my lungs open wide like I've bounded from the lake. I crack the window, though my breath puffs in front of me, and wait for a sound to ping from next door. Max's chuckle, a girl's voice. The outside world filling my cold, dark house with life. But silence is all I hear.

Balling up on the floor beside my bed, I fold a piece of bread in half. Lettuce presses into the dough, and when I bite the middle of the bread, the leaf crunches. After my parents fall asleep, Mom on the couch with Cirrus in her lap, Dad passed out in bed still wearing his boots, I'll tiptoe to the kitchen for something else to eat. I imagine Mom knocking on my door, offering a hug, asking me to go with her to pick up Grace from Dr. Nelson's. We could stop by Plum Lake Café and order burgers and sweet potato fries. Imagining a hot meal at the table, together, makes me smile.

I tear a chunk of bread, squish it into a ball between my fingers as the moisture from the lettuce saturates the dough. I close my eyes, pop the hunk of sandwich into my mouth, and almost taste bacon grease mixed with marinara. Lucio & Sons Picasso Pizza Pies.

I allow my mind to wander into Max's house, his living room, kitchen, and bedroom. The spaces we shared together. I miss him. I miss us. But when I think of the pizza he's sharing with someone else, my eyes pop open, and my stomach aches. Thoughts of Max with someone else hurt, though months have passed and we've both moved on. I suppose I didn't expect Max to move on the way he did. Maybe I should start parading guys through the driveway Friday afternoons and make a show of how we, too, have the house to ourselves.

Cirrus mews at the door, and my chest tightens. Within seconds the engine roars outside my window.

Shit! Dad's home.

4

MAX

SHOUTS BOOM FROM THE PORCH. Pawtrick Swayze hits his doggy door on cue and barks. He loops the driveway, back legs slipping as he races toward the steps and sits next to me on the porch. I wrap my arm around his chubby torso and hug him.

Most nights between seven and eight o'clock, noise echoes from Aggi's house. Exact words never form, at least I can't make them out, but sound ricochets off tree trunks and the chipped white walls holding up the Frank home. I tuck my knees to my chest and brush snowflakes off my snow pants. Shoveling the already-shoveled snow distracts me for a few minutes but doesn't distance me from the painful reality of Aggi and me no longer speaking.

My stomach growls, and I regret not eating the pizza. When my parents go to bed, I'll pop a few slices in the microwave and feast, but now my eyes are fixed on the house next door.

Aggi's window above the garage is a swollen black eye and I wish it would open, show light, and tell me Aggi's safe, but she's never at her desk when the yelling begins. I imagine her locked in the bathroom or tucked safely in bed. Sometimes, when shoveling snow isn't enough to clear my head, I run to the dock, and by the time I return, I envision myself marching up the Frank front steps, pounding the door, and interrupting their argument. There are repercussions and danger with this fantasy, and I'd probably mess up the wrongful-death lawsuit my dad filed against Aggi's family, but in that brief moment of strength, I care nothing about a civil harassment restraining order. I only care about Aggi.

After Aggi's dad pinned mine against one of the refrigeration trucks they co-owned for the family business, smashed his face into the hood, it was only reasonable for my father to demand I call the cops. Except Aggi's dad is practically one of them, or he was. After Mr. Frank finished his day job working side by side with my dad, he used to ride in police cars Friday and Saturday nights, playing pretend cop to kids like Henry with a family history of breaking the law. Aggi's dad, like other cops in this town of seven hundred people, worked as a volunteer—a reserve police officer—with a heart to serve. I used to see the charitable heart worn on the sleeve of Mr. Frank's blue button-up. He took pride in his volunteer work, and my brother, Cal, and I looked up to him when Mr. Frank talked about making a difference, but now all I see are his empty eyes, and all I hear are his harsh words. Aggi's dad hasn't worn his police uniform since he used his cop moves on my father. Arms twisted. Face planted. My dad calling out for help. After the incident, Mr. Frank was immediately removed from his volunteer position with the police force, and he quit showing up to work with my dad.

I remember Aggi's dad shouting that my father could not possibly grasp the loss he felt. Kate, dying the way she did. Cal's death, instantaneous. According to Mr. Frank, somehow, Cal's death should be easier on us.

I've considered his words. In bed, they play on a loop until I drown them out with music. Mr. Frank's reasoning is tainted with his own pain and heartbreak, but when you grow up respecting a person like he's your own father, the words twist around in your brain until you're confused.

Even now I think about Mr. Frank's words. When my parents ask me to join them on the couch for popcorn and comedy—Mom and Dad watch a lot of TV and eat a hell of a lot of popcorn—I remember what Aggi's dad said and wonder how my parents can laugh at the comedians and sprinkle sweet toppings on their corn. Shouldn't they be crying? Tonight they sit on the couch, staring blankly at the television, while Aggi's parents argue. My parents never fight, and the only time they cried was during my brother's funeral. They haven't shed a tear since. I wish I knew why they watch so much TV.

Aggi's parents fight for thirty minutes. Pawtrick tumbles down the steps to pee in the snow but returns to huddle next to me with ears perked. He's listening for Aggi's voice, too, but I don't hear it. My stomach churns but not from hunger.

"Hey, Son." I jump and whip around. Dad's leaning against the doorframe. "Want to catch the basketball game? Your mother went to bed early." He yawns, his eyes forcibly wide.

I shrug. "Homework." A lie.

He flicks on the porch light. "Well, you should probably come in."

Silence.

"And if you change your mind, you know where I'll be." *On the couch, stuffing your cheeks with popcorn, trotting along the hamster wheel of life.*

"Sure, Dad." I lift my finger, turn back around to face the drive. "I know where to find you."

Dad hesitates on the porch. I glance over my shoulder. He's staring at Aggi's house, and I follow his gaze bouncing from window to window as lights pops off, the house shutting its eyes.

After a few seconds, Dad sighs. "Grace is with Dr. Nelson. Saw her leave last Sunday night."

I mumble, "Yeah, well, Aggi's still in there."

His nostrils flare as he closes his eyes and nods. "There's nothing we can do, Max." He backs inside the open door. "Not our business anymore." Dad squeezes the door shut.

My eyes fixate on Aggi's house as I mull Dad's words over in my brain, my mouth. *Not our business anymore.* The kitchen light pops on for ten seconds. I count. Then the room blackens. I disagree with everything my dad says.

5

Aggi

BY EIGHT THIRTY MY MOTHER folds on the couch, clutching her phone and swiping through pictures of Kate. Between sobs, she calls out memories so painful to hear that I reach into my pocket in search of my earbuds. I pop them in but leave the music on mute to monitor their argument from the stairs.

Mom needs comfort. Hugs and hands held. I want to snuggle beside her, drape my arm over her shoulders, and drop my chin into the curve of her neck, where it's warm and smells like flowers and mint. But she pushed Grace away and refuses eye contact with me. Dad sits nearby, nursing his fourth bottle of beer, which means he's loud and unpredictable and won't leave Mom alone. As soon as she leans toward the coffee table to pour a glass of wine, he harps about her drinking. By

Mom's second glass, he's skinning her cooking and cleaning, too. Dad never used to care that Mom didn't have time for mundane tasks. They shared household duties while Mom took classes tuition-free. She was earning a business degree that would help her move from administrative support to office manager. "Killing two birds with one stone," she said with a wink. When she applied for the job opening as administrative assistant in the biology department at the university twenty-some miles south of town, Mom's mission was to help her family. The new job would allow Kate to go to college tuition-free, once Mom had been employed for two years. If I chose the same school, and of course I would because there was no way I could afford college otherwise, I'd also attend tuition-free.

Mom, always learning, willing to improve life for her family. She didn't need a college education to prove herself to us. She was as bright as the stars. Ask her anything, and if she didn't have the answer, which was rare, she'd find the answer, and guide you along on the journey to discover it for yourself. But you can't ask Mom questions now. Answers are buried below layers of hurt. After Kate died, Mom withdrew from her classes with no plans to return to school, in spite of Dr. Nelson's persistent begging.

She still works, unlike Dad, but only enough hours to keep the power company from shutting off our lights. I haven't asked for anything new in months. Shampoo, razors, mouthwash. I don't make much money working in Dr. Nelson's lab, but it's enough for incidentals. Half my paycheck I spend on gas so I can travel back and forth to the college, but it's worth every penny if it keeps me out of the house.

"She was seven," Mom moans, "when she turned the back-yard into a nature preserve. Remember that, James? Are you listening?" Mom shouts now, even though Dad has moved beside her on the couch. "Seven! Kate did things differently from the other kids. Remember?" Mom's words slur, and she sips more wine.

"I remember everything!"

"I don't think you do!" Mom snaps. "That's what happens when time passes. We forget details."

A year ago, my mother, Queen of Details, balanced work with school, made sure the Crock-Pot dinged at six o'clock with something delicious, and left Dad love notes, which he matched with chicken-scratch letters and bubble hearts. Our house ticked along like a fine-tuned clock. The gentle rap of a hammer or the circular saw cutting along penciled lines on wood as Dad rushed to finish a project on the house before Mom got home from work or class. Mom and Dad balanced each other. Both carried their own weight. Every-thing's tilted now.

Sitting on the wooden stairs, my gray jeans collecting year-old sawdust, I draw my knees to my chest and wonder when life will improve. I know it will never return to how it was, but I consider the length of time it will take Mom to stop with-holding hugs and kisses from her living daughters. When Dad will quit blaming everyone for his problems. Like if Mom doesn't do a goddamn load of laundry, the sun won't shine.

"Enough wine." Dad fumbles the stem of Mom's wineglass and it tips, rolls, crashes onto the plywood where new hardwood should be. "Goddammit! See what you made me do?"

Feet shuffle. A thud. "Ouch!"

"You've had enough to drink."

Sure, Dad. Tell Mom she's had enough; tell her she's falling apart. Tell her she should handle her grief by following your lead.

"A mother shouldn't have to bury her child!" my mother groans.

I rock back and forth on the step.

"A father shouldn't have to bury *his* little girl!" Dad shouts, as if Mom's to blame.

The tug-of-war never stops. Back and forth, back and forth. My parents refused to pause long enough to plan Kate's funeral. Arrangements belonged to me, and I sorted through them with Dr. Nelson's help. I didn't think twice about responsibility or who should handle what. It was the least I could do for my sister. Kate would have done the same for me. After reading the literature the hospital gave us, I made phone calls, chose the clothes my sister loved and would be buried in, and wrote her obituary. I stayed up all night writing, reading aloud, crossing out lines, and starting again. One typo, as though a bird shit on top of your newly washed car.

Dad's voice booms. "Look at this place!" More thuds, and an empty box launches across the room. "When do you plan to clean up this mess?"

Thin walls surround me in our dilapidated lakefront farm-house, especially since renovations braked and layers of pink insulation fell onto the floor. Our forever home now temporary, according to the mortgage company. Mom's paycheck doesn't cover the house payment, but at least she still has a job and didn't quit after striking a colleague (Max's dad) and threatening his son (Max). Have I mentioned my father has turned into the world's biggest asshole?

According to the grief counselor at the hospital, we are a normal family facing abnormal circumstances. A punch line I remember from therapy—day one. My father quit when Max's parents sued us. He filed a counterclaim the next day and now occupies his hours with a costly lawsuit destined to put us on the streets. Who has time for a job when you're busy fighting with your best friend, staking flags in your piece of land, and standing your ground? It turns out blame consumes a hell of a lot of time.

I scoot to the landing and quietly push myself to my feet. As I tiptoe toward my room, Cirrus cuts me off in the hall, darting into the bathroom tub. Her senses acute, head tilted, ears perked. I step past the door and flip on the light switch so she won't have to sit in the dark. When I round the corner, I trip over a two-by-four leaning against the wall, and it slaps the bare floor, sending particles of dust into orbit.

"Aggi? Get down here!"

I leap across the hallway and squeeze my door shut before darting into bed, sliding into the middle, and wrapping the covers over my head. Within seconds my dad's boots stomp the wood, shake the walls. I close my eyes so tight my face scrunches, then begin to count. At eight, Dad swings open my bedroom door and it slams against the wall. Three books domino on the shelf; one hits the floor with a thud.

Dad grunts and flips on the light.

"Didn't you hear me call you?" His voice is heavy and loud. The only tool left in my tactical bag of home survival gear is pretend sleeping, so I don't move, but he does.

"Aggi!" He bumps the mattress. The covers fan me as they're peeled from the bed. "What are you doing?"

Fear tightens its grip around my throat. "Sleeping." My voice squeaks.

Dad tosses the comforter over me and stomps to my desk. He rakes his fingers through the blinds, grabs the window, slams it to the sill, and flips the latch. I curl into a tight ball.

"Bastard," he mumbles.

Maybe now I should run. Race out the back door and haul ass for the lake. I could be on the dock in minutes. Staring at the stars, making wishes I once believed could come true. Kate and I used to race to the dock. She'd pop her head into my room and say, "Cal and Max are heading to the lake. Let's go! Last one there has to row the canoe!" It'd take me ten seconds to meet her on the porch, with or without shoes. "Race you!" she'd shout, bounding the steps and sprinting across the driveway. "No fair!" I'd shout, but she was already on the path to the lake, her long legs impossible to outpace.

35

"James?" Mom calls from the hall in her high-pitched pinot-noir voice. I really miss her mom voice. Sweet and less bitter. "I'm going to bed."

"They should move!" Dad shouts, and paws the blinds. He whips around and knocks his hip against my chair. "Them! Not us!"

Dad aims his bloodshot eyes at me. I stare at his face, then his feet, and fish for earbuds stuffed beneath my pillow as Dad steps closer to my bed. His words, when they wind up and shoot, kick me in the gut and leave me breathless. I understand Dad is angry—we all are—but his anger is misdirected, and it's turned into something dark and meaningless, something set on destruction.

"They need to pay for what they did. Don't you agree?" Dad drops onto my bed and stares at his boots.

I want to speak softly and tell Dad that everyone is paying, but he insists the Grangers are to blame for my sister's death. Complications arose when Dad pushed Max's father's face into their work truck. According to Dad, he did what he had to do. But the timeline is fuzzy. I know Max's dad was the first to file a lawsuit against my family, but I'm unclear if it was before or after their fight. As terrible as my father has become, it's hard to blame him after the hell he's been through. He was the one to find his daughter dead.

Mom stumbles into my room, her hips wrapped in a decade-old Chanel skirt my grandmother sent from Connecticut a couple of weeks before she passed. The silver clip in Mom's hair slides when she rolls her neck. Wrinkles dip at the sides of her lipstick-smudged mouth and the starfish at the corners of her eyes etch into her skin deeper now than last week.

"That lawsuit will break us until we have nothing left." Mom leans against the door, and I straighten my spine.

"Dignity," Dad says. "That's what we'll have. And it's what Kate deserves."

Max's parents set the wrongful death suit in motion. They say my sister was to blame for Cal's death, and my dad is suing them for the pain he says drove my sister to harm herself. The paperwork doesn't mention Max or me, but it really should. Had I not been tearing Max's clothes from his body, had we caged our hormones for even a minute the night his brother died, none of this would have happened. I am to blame for my sister's death.

Mom's shoulders dip. Her knees bend. I feel my muscles tighten as I wait for her rebuttal.

"We moved here first," Dad says. "This property belonged to us before it belonged to them."

"Sure," Mom says with a sigh, her head falling against the door. "Why don't you march over there and tell them to move. That's what you want. Right?"

Mom glances in my direction, and my eyes widen. Is she seeing me?

"It won't do any good," she says, her gaze falling to the floor. "Won't bring our Kate back."

For a moment, the room quiets and the only sound wafts in from the hallway as Cirrus braves a swift exit from the bathroom. Dad and I sit on my bed. Mom tilts against the door. I live for these seconds of silence when we inhale and exhale in rhythm. The pause allows us to visit familiar places. The rug in the center of my room where Grace curled her body around Cirrus. The chair at my desk where Kate strummed her guitar and sang lyrics she and Cal had written earlier in the day. When we stop and listen, we hear hope.

But Dad stands and ruins the silence. "You better not be speaking to that boy, Aggi!" He points. "You hear me?"

The whole woods hears you, Dad.

"Because if I catch you talking to him . . ." Pop in earbuds. Amp volume. Dad's lips flap, but I no longer hear him. I can't. I won't. I refuse.

THE HARDEST DAYS

Lyrics by Kate Frank and Cal Granger

When the sun won't shine like you thought it would
When the rain won't spill like you think it should
When he smiles and you don't see
When she walks away from where you thought she'd be

The hardest days are when you lose your way
When parts of your heart tear
And you hang on to what scared
You yesterday more than today

And tomorrow
When fear pushes you away
And the distance grows
Between you and hope

These are the ways
These are the days
When nothing's left but memories
Pain and hurt and other things

These are the hardest days
These are the hardest days

6

ON SATURDAY MORNINGS I DRIVE twenty-five miles to the nearest college and run laps at a track reserved for collegiate athletes, which I am wholeheartedly not, but nobody questions me, so I'm beginning to believe I look the part. For the record, running sucks, or maybe I suck at running, especially after gorging myself at midnight with pizza soaked in bacon grease.

But exercise is not what lures me onto campus.

Aggi's here.

Washing test tubes, sweeping the lab, sneaking up to the roof of the science building to tinker with the weather station. Before the accident, Aggi obsessed over weather. She lived for Doppler radar graphs, thrived on atmospheric readings, always challenging herself to predict storm patterns before the news reported them. But weather in North Carolina is unpredictable. Ice storms happen when snow's predicted. Lightning strikes when sprinkles are expected. And when it's snowing in Walabash Woods, ice might pummel the ground in a nearby city. Aggi and I learned how unstable the weather is the hard way, and since the accident, I haven't seen Aggi on the roof of the science building. But today I'm hopeful.

A breeze stirs the top layer of snow into the air, and I puff the ice crystals from my bangs and lift my left arm to open up my lungs. By lap two, I'm gasping for air. My nonrunner friend Henry told me running gets easier the more you do it, but I find this statement to be a bald-faced lie. My cleats dig and punch holes into patches of snow spotting the track.

When I skid around a curve, the eaves of the science building poke through the leafless trees, and for a second, my breath catches, my heart drums. I squint at the windows to search for movement. Just a glimpse is all I need. Aggi's blue knit hat, her sand-colored hair sweeping her forehead.

Aggi used to work only one day a month, but now she arrives every Saturday morning and some weekday afternoons. Filling up my Jeep costs a small fortune and drains my meager savings account. Dad would lend me money if I asked, but it feels wrong, as if I am breaking our father-son trust. The restraining order prevents my family from speaking to Aggi's family, yet here I am following her around like Edward stalked Bella. Aggi loves *Twilight*, and quite frankly, so do I, but at least I'm not sleep stalking . . . yet? A million court documents try to keep me from Aggi, but life is not worth living without her.

Along the three-quarter-mile curve, I sniff my armpits and slow to a bouncy walk. I need to be careful not to break the boundaries between sweat and wintry air, when my sweat glands open and seep salt through my shirt. Today, I parked my Jeep in the same lot as Aggi's car, making it quite possible for me to bump into her when I—*we*—leave campus. Can't be smelling of skunk, now, can I?

I won't physically bump into Aggi. Not with a restraining order in full force. Although I'm not sure the court order applies to me, to Aggi, when we're away from our common land, I'd rather not test Aggi's father. He's more frightening than any restraining order. Mr. Frank's become a larger-than-life asteroid, aimed at the earth, ready to blow it apart with his anger. He has me head-checking when I leave the house, looking over my shoulder for a lurking shadow. And to make matters worse, Aggi's mom has been wandering the campus more than usual, and even on a Saturday. Last week, she nearly saw me. I darted behind the brick wall of the library when she passed, wiping her eyes and mumbling to herself. She looked lost, and my heart broke for her. I wanted to jog beside her, put my arm around her, and say, *Hey, Mrs. F., I miss our talks, your laughs at my terrible jokes, and your peach cobbler. My mom misses you, too.* But that would have caused problems for everyone.

One last head-check to make sure nobody's following me,

and I head for the science building. A rock wall separates the library from Aggi's building and provides the perfect place for fake pull-ups. Gawkers are nonexistent in college, or so it seems. Nobody gives a shit what you do. Everyone minds their own business, unlike in high school, where everyone talks to everyone else and spreads more rumor than fact. Once in a while a college girl walks by, but I don't pay attention. I'm here for one reason: Aggi.

After my fourth pull-up, my biceps and shoulders burn. Last year, my grandmother called me string bean, and girls avoided me like bad breath. This year, since I started working out, the whole world notices. Well, that's the lie I tell myself. When your brother's best friend kills him in a car accident, small-town fame swirls around you like those whirlpool clouds Aggi used to obsess over.

I heave myself onto the retaining wall and hang. After a few seconds, someone moves past the window.

Oh, God. It's her.

Wearing a gray-and-white gravity-defying ski cap on the back of her head, she turns, talking to someone. A student? Professor? I squint to study Aggi's body language. Loose, relaxed. She's talking with her hands. I hope not to a guy. An older, bigger-chested college guy. I drop to the cement, hunch over, and grip my knees. Hard to breathe when your girlfriend—*ex*-girlfriend—is talking to a college guy. He's probably *really* into science and weather, too, and cracks college-guy jokes. Blessed with an epic beard and good humor. I can already hear him with his *Why is sex like a thunderstorm?* bit.

I rub the back of my neck as someone says, "Hey." A guy in thick-framed glasses and a goddamned cape. College students. Doing their own shit their own way since forever. What I wouldn't give to do that, instead of hanging on a retaining wall, scraping my elbows and knees, while the love of my life washes test tubes and listens to bad weather jokes.

But this is my life since Cal died. Since guilt killed Aggi's sister.

Two deaths in less than one month. Grief took its toll on both families. Aggi's parents visited the same hell mine did and still do. Aggi's parents are mad, hurt, and I get it. They blame us. Isn't that what people do when tragedy hits? Search for answers, even if it means pointing fingers? At least my family didn't have to walk in on a loved one hanging lifeless in their bedroom. At least we didn't have to hear the thud of Kate's body hitting hardwood when Aggi's dad cut his own belt from his daughter's neck. My family has painful memories, too, but sometimes the good stomp away the bad.

When I think about the suffering Aggi's family has endured, I get mad, too. I want to scream that it was a fucking accident. It wasn't like Kate lost control of her car on purpose. They were both wearing seat belts. Neither drinking. Kate didn't choose to take my brother's life any more than she chose to take her own. A horrible accident followed by suffering.

But then the lawyers started visiting at dinnertime. My dad

began acting shifty, quit making eye contact with me and my mom. He'd motion for a guy in a suit and tie and slick black cowboy boots to meet him in his truck; then they'd drive around the lake. Planning, plotting, him eating up whatever they were selling. They talked money. That's what this is really about. All those whispers of wrongful death. Murmurings of pain and suffering and who's responsible for hospital bills. I want to ask my dad what price his friendship has. Whether it's worth losing his best friend. He's already lost a son.

Now all that's left is blame and a shit-ton of paperwork.

All I want is for life to go back to the way it once was. When our parents were best friends. When I had two families, not one. When my brother, Cal, sat on the porch plucking at his guitar, humming melodies and strumming chords with Kate. When I knew Aggi loved me and we didn't have to pretend not to see each other when our parents were watching. And that's what I'm the least certain of: if Aggi still feels the way she felt that afternoon on the lake when she shouted that she loved me so loud the entire woods stopped to listen. Does Aggi feel the same way about my family, about me, as her father does? And if so, would I blame her? My dad's responsible for this mess. Isn't he?

My brain buzzes with confusion. Scratches on my elbows will heal, but my heart, Aggi's heart, might vaporize into nothing unless we fight to rebuild the broken pieces before it's too late.

I throw myself at the retaining wall and grapple with the

45

stone until my body hangs in a semicomfortable position.

Aggi. In the window. A figure steps beside her, and I recognize Dr. Nelson's brushless-since-the-eighties hair. Aggi pulls her hat from her head and digs her hand into her curls, turns, and disappears into the lab.

"She's there," I say out loud, and shake my arms free of cramps.

When I turn around, a girl on a bench lifts her bushy eyebrow and nods.

I scowl, growl even, but not at the girl. It's all this shit in my head. I want to talk to Aggi so bad it hurts. I want to wait for her outside the science building and ask if she still loves me. I want to tell her how I resisted the lawsuit, threatened to never speak to my father again if he went through with it. But most of all, I want to say I'm sorry.

I hike myself up onto the rock wall and plant my chin on the ledge. Aggi floats by the window, wiping fog from the glass. Her face pink, lips red and full. If I concentrate, close my eyes and focus, her lips brush against mine. A warm-sugar-cookie taste. Aggi stares in my direction, and for a split second I'm flooded with hope, wondering if she sees me hanging here, but then I freak. My arms weaken, feet scramble against the stone. A couple of feet above ground, and it feels like parkour training on the side of a skyscraper. All four limbs flail, and I drop, my chin dragging over the flagstone, my mouth tasting of metal.

"Fuck!" I shout as my ankle rolls and my ass hits the ground.

Aggi saw me. Now what do I do?

"You good?" the girl on the bench asks.

Twisting around, I brush the gravel stuck to my palms and knees and mumble, "No. Never."

The girl walks toward me and extends a hand. "You sure you're okay?"

My cheeks burn, chin stings. "Nope," I say. "There is nothing okay about me." I flip the hood of my sweatshirt over my head. If only I had that college guy's cape, I would swing it in front of me for an unparalleled dramatic exit.

7

Aggi

MAX THINKS I DON'T KNOW he follows me to work and watches me from the library. "'Stalks' is more like it," Umé said after I told her I saw Max at the college. Four times. "If you don't like it, call him out on that shit," she insisted. But my feelings for Max swing like a pendulum. One moment Max parades girls in front of my house and I'm confused why he feels the need to flaunt his grief recovery in that way, and the next he sits on his porch and stares at my window, or checks up on me at work. According to the thesaurus app on my phone, a stalker harasses someone with *unwanted* attention. I'm unsure what I want. A part of me believes Max still cares about us, about what was taken from us, but so much has happened since his brother's funeral. Maybe Max and his feelings ride the same pendulum.

The first time I noticed Max following me to work was when I saw his Jeep in the parking lot. Max has no reason to visit the college campus, so my curiosity steered me alongside his Jeep. I hoped I'd see something on the seat or the dash that would hint at what Max was up to. What I did not expect to find was Max flat on his back, practically stuffed beneath the steering wheel, hair sticking straight up like a hedgehog. I sprinted across the lot before our eyes connected.

The next time I noticed Max darting around campus like a cartoon spy, he was jogging on the sidewalk, long arms dangling at his side, knees barely bending with each step. I mean, Max, jogging? The same boy who insisted he had the lungs of a thirty-year smoker every time I beat him in a race for the dock. Max cut across the sidewalk and hesitated, pivoted, then darted in the other direction. I wanted to shout, *Max! I see you! I totally see you!* but I froze. A part of me, the part I push away out of fear, wants Max to keep his distance. From afar, he's safe. But the selfish part of me wants Max to watch me. At least then I know he still cares. That selfish part of who I am scares me. It's the part that could get Max in trouble and me blamed even more than I already am. Dad blames Max and me for the accident. And most days, I suppose I do, too.

On weekend mornings, the campus snoozes except for a few students laughing as they pilgrimage to the library. As the minutes tick by, small pockets of college kids leave their dorms for breakfast in the dining hall. I stare out the window

49

of the biology lab and smile to myself, imagining all the fun they're having. They laugh, hold hands, as they march around campus. When I pass students on intersecting sidewalks, they always say hello, and I pretend to be a friendly person, too, like my life is full and rich and uncomplicated. Like I'm happy to be alive.

Kate would be a freshman this year. A double major in math and music. That was her plan.

I think a lot about Kate when I walk to Dr. Nelson's lab and stare out over the campus courtyard. I imagine my sister racing toward me on a sidewalk, stopping to ruffle my hair, then bolting to the music room to practice piano before meeting friends for melon and eggs (her two favorite foods). All those shades of yellow and orange, she used to say, like someone scooped the sun and made freezer pops.

Saturday mornings, when I stroll by oak trees dipped in white and girls in oversized sweaters, my thoughts wrap around Kate. What her daily routine would be like. Would she return to the music room after breakfast in the commons, or would she swing home to do a load of laundry before hitting the books? I imagine her stopping by the house on a sleepy Sunday morning with an oversized bag full of dirty clothes hiked onto her back as she shoves the door open with her foot. Her long, dark hair spilling over one shoulder, sunglasses pushed high on her head.

Kate promised she wouldn't forget me while she was away at school. All twenty-five miles away. Some people travel the country so they can attend college far from family, but not Kate. She said a small public institution in a neighboring city suited her just fine, but I know the tuition waiver my mom received as a benefit for working at the university was the real reason.

"You're here early for a Saturday." I make my way to the autoclave—the high-pressure steamer I use to sterilize glassware—and fumble with the buttons until the engine whirls.

Dr. Nelson squats in front of an aquarium rigged for bees. "Grace wanted to go out for breakfast, so we stopped here first. Had to check on my other children, too." Dr. Nelson taps the glass with her fingertip and smiles.

Tanks containing flowers native to North Carolina line the lab walls, but two containers buzz with bees that belong in some Scandinavian country. The bees, just one of the many mysteries surrounding Dr. Nelson and her lab. I used to ask my mother how Helsinki bees ended up in a western North Carolina laboratory, but Mom whispered, "Dr. Nelson is strict with her *don't ask, don't tell* policy." Every time one of her students inquires, Dr. Nelson lowers her voice and references Victor Frankenstein, Doctor Griffin, Lex Luthor.

Since working in the lab, I've learned to ask questions Dr. Nelson *will* answer, and I've learned a lot about these small, solitary bees with leaf-cutter relatives, known as *Chelostoma florisomne*. These little creatures used to make me squeamish, but after spending hours online reading Dr. Nelson's publications on how weather impacts bee behavior, I've fallen in love with these damn insects, and with Dr. Nelson, too.

Weather patterns were once my specialty. Predicting them was what I was good at. Call me competitive, but I had to know what the sky planned to do to us before it had a chance to do it. Before the accident, I spent a lot of time learning to predict unpredictable weather.

"Is Gracie with you?" I crane my neck toward the door.

Dr. Nelson turns from the tank. "She's in my office playing on the computer. Didn't think you'd be here so early. Want to join us for breakfast?"

I imagine Max somewhere on campus and snatch a towel from its hook, rub the numbers off an Erlenmeyer flask. "Should probably stay here. The lab's a wreck."

Dr. Nelson's eyes dart around the neat and tidy room, and her eyebrows lift.

"I'll be here all day cleaning. Tomorrow, too, if you don't mind me clocking Sunday hours."

Dr. Nelson detects my reluctance to leave the lab. "Need more time out of the house, huh?"

Dr. Nelson, Mom's boss-turned-confidante, knows my family better than I do. She is responsible for Mom going back to school to finish a degree she started decades ago. She's seen my mother at her best, then witnessed her falling apart.

"Just thought, you know, I'm here Saturdays anyway. May as well make a weekend out of it." I shut off the water.

Dr. Nelson clamps one hand to her hip; the other pushes

at her conditioner-less locks. She's poised to speak but only listens.

"Mom could really use the hours." I'm pushing the desperation button, and I almost feel guilty as Dr. Nelson won't be able to resist.

After Kate died, Mom cut her hours at the college, and I offered to step in and help. Mom, crumbling before us, tried to go to work, get out of the house and maintain some semblance of a routine, but several mornings she'd drive right past the campus and end up in a Target parking lot on the other side of town. She'd cut the engine and sit alone in the car for hours, shivering when I'd find her. Dr. Nelson called morning after morning worried, asking what time my mother left for work. Weeks of Mom's late shows and absences turned to months. Dr. Nelson didn't have the heart to report Mom missing work. Legally speaking, Dr. Nelson could get into trouble, but morally speaking, Dr. Nelson doesn't have two shits to give. So Dr. Nelson clocks some of Mom's meager hours as though Mom worked them, except I do. Dr. Nelson and I have an understanding, and we never talk about it. *Don't ask, don't tell.* I'm just happy to be out of the house, away from Dad, who is also crumbling before us.

"I suppose these guys could benefit from Sunday data readings," Dr. Nelson says with a wink.

I dry my hands on a towel and walk toward the bees shooting around the tank. Their unpredictable movements remind me how order-less life is even though science says otherwise.

A bee slams against the plastic, buzzing at high pitch, and I flinch.

"Maybe I should stick to cleaning. Neaten your desk. Sing to the plants."

Dr. Nelson smiles. "These beauties are harmless. You know they won't sting. But you have to know how to handle them."

My eyes widen. "Handle them?"

Dr. Nelson chuckles. "I'm only kidding." She pats my back. Her hand pauses, then moves to my shoulder and squeezes.

"Parents still fucking with your brain?"

I nod, purse my lips, a signal that shit, also known as my life, is the same today as it was yesterday, but I'd rather not go into details.

Dr. Nelson's head drops, as she recognizes the same-shit pattern when she sees it.

"Why don't you start Sunday shifts tomorrow."

I exhale. "Thank you. But what if Grace begs to come home?" I worry my little sister will be alone with Mom and Dad, and I won't be there to protect her from hearing or see-ing something anxiety-inducing.

Dr. Nelson shakes her head. "Oh, no. She's not going to be there if you're not. I'll keep her with me."

Grace skips through the door, shouting, "When are we going to eat? I'm starving!" When she sees me, she tilts her head, squeezes one eye shut, like she's examining me, assess-ing if I'm okay. I flash a smile and wave, and her shoulders melt, air releasing from her tightly wound body. I open my arms, but she turns toward Dr. Nelson.

"Hang in there, kiddo." Dr. Nelson pats my shoulder and leans in toward my ear. "Someday, your dad will realize his mistakes, blame himself, and beg the universe for forgiveness."

I hope Dr. Nelson is right.

As I walk through the parking lot, I stare at my phone. Now that I'm aware Max lurks around campus, I don't want him to see me seeing him. I wonder what Max is up to besides hiding in his car, climbing the retaining wall at the library, and sprinting down the sidewalk when he thinks I've spotted him.

If I hadn't seen Max hanging on the library wall, I would have thought he showed up on campus to exercise, run laps, do something to occupy his time. I thought, for a hot minute, that running could be Max's new hobby, a much-needed distraction, and I smiled thinking how alike the two of us are. How I stroll through campus remembering Kate. Maybe Max, too, visits the college to clear his head or connect with memories of his brother. But then I figured out running is Max's excuse to spy on me.

The paperwork preventing Max and me from speaking complicates my life. If only we could talk. In a perfect world, where Dad didn't check my phone to see if I'd "broken trust" and contacted Max, I could ask Maxwell Granger why the hell he parades girls he barely knows through my driveway and into his house to do God knows what. This new hobby of Max's, which conveniently started after Max and I were together, reaches far beyond the therapy of running. Why does Max shove his dating life in my face and then follow me to work? The juxtaposition of that boy's actions makes me want to scream. I quash my feelings for Max, or at least try, but my thoughts meander long enough to imagine what he does with the girls he brings home. Things we used to do.

Last year, before crash (BC), Max met me on campus and we explored places students weren't allowed to visit without professors or permission. We found the rooftop weather station together. I knew it existed, somewhere, and I'd asked my mother about it for months, but Max was the one who convinced me to search. Like it was a hidden treasure.

Max insisted we explore the entire science building until we located the station, and when we did, he said, "This would make the perfect spot . . ."

"For what?" I asked as his cheeks blazed.

Max shrugged. "You know."

I suppose I did. We'd been discussing it for weeks. Even made a list of pros and cons—mostly pros written by me—and had done some serious planning. The roof turned out to be the backdrop for our first attempt at sex. And by attempt, I mean no matter how much we planned, there was still a lot of poking and jabbing and *I'm sorry, I don't know what I'm doing.* All my firsts have been with Max. His firsts with me. Then our world crashed and everything stopped. Our love, frozen in time.

Five bumpers in front of me I spot Max's Jeep and his staggered parking job. Either Max is trying to hide his vehicle by parking out of the lines, or the snow conceals boundaries and lines he didn't see. Since Max's Jeep is white, he probably thinks it's camouflaged.

I cut to the opposite side of the lot to avoid seeing Max again back-flat on the seat. I'm four car lengths from the Jeep when I hear panting, someone struggling for air. I slow my pace, pivot sideways, and crouch behind a car. When the panting stops, I stand and whip to the side of the vehicle as Max darts behind an oak tree. *How incredibly cliché.*

Max wearing black running tights, but missing the runner's legs. Two toothpicks swimming in a sea of basketball shorts.

Since we were kids, I've poked fun at Max in an affectionate way, and right now I want to shout: *You should have worn white, Max! Camouflage, even! You stick out in the snow like Pawtrick Swayze's turds!* Instead, I whisper, "I see you, Maxwell Granger. I totally see you."

8

MAX

AGGI DOESN'T SEE ME. HOW could she? I'm fast as a snowshoe hare. I regret wearing all black, though. What was I thinking? My heart pounds as I watch Aggi. Her back is all I see, but my body floats like a bubble, and then, instant heart palpitations. Her head drops forward, hair spills across her ears and face. I can't lift my eyes from her until I catch myself staring at her ass. I mean, it's covered beneath her coat, so I can't actually see it, but I imagine how superb it looks, and then I feel like I shouldn't be looking.

The small parking lot, layered with fresh snow, hushes, and Aggi's voice whispers in the distance. A mumble, incoherent words, but enough of a sound to make me smile. Aggi, always talking to herself. I'd give anything to hear her voice again at my ear. *I love you, Max.*

It's impossible not to think of our last moments together on the rooftop of the science building, kissing, unbuttoning shirts, whispering how much we wanted each other. I tried to act like I knew what I was doing. Mister Experience. But Aggi knew better. All discoveries were made with Aggi next to me. First steps, first bicycle ride, first swim in the lake.

I lean forward from behind the tree trunk and steal another glance. Aggi's shutting her car door. The engine hums, but instead of backing out and taking the immediate exit on her right, she whips left and circles the long way around the lot. She's headed toward me, lights on bright. *What the hell is she doing?*

I leap toward the tree, my feet slipping on takeoff before sinking into calf-deep snow. Behind me, perched on top of the powder, sits my damn shoe.

Aggi's car creeps through the parking lot. My toes tingle from my soaking sock.

I spin on one foot, shift sideways, suck in my stomach, and deflate my chest. The latter is impossible, of course.

The car engine purrs, and I can't tell if Aggi's stopped or is backing up. I wonder if she saw me. A head-check can't hurt.

Gripping the tree trunk with both arms, I slide my upper body to one side, then shoot my neck out like a turtle for a quick glance. The engine revs. My eyes widen. Aggi hits the gas and chunks of snow and slush launch in my direction. A dollop whacks my forehead as I grapple with the tree, cursing my fingerless gloves. My hands slip, face splats against the

59

trunk. My arms, weak from hanging on the retaining wall, refuse to hold and I fall backward. Instant snow angel.

Snow caves around my silhouette as I lift my head and back, and climb to my feet. Aggi's car fishtails out of the parking lot and onto the road. She couldn't have seen me. My body moved before my mind caught up, but that spinout seemed on cue. As if Aggi knew I was hiding behind the tree. I pat my pants. The Aggi I know would never do something like that on purpose. An avalanche of feelings slams into me I don't know Aggi anymore. It's been months since we last spoke.

9

Aggi

MAX SUCKS AT STALKING. AND that fall? Oh my God.
For a split second, the urge to stop the car and help him out
of the snow overwhelmed me, but now I think of Grace no
longer living at home, of Dr. Nelson insisting Dad will one
day blame himself and not me, and of Max bringing girls to
his house nearly every week. I slap the steering wheel. Max
doesn't follow me because he still cares about us; he's gathering information to use against my family. My stomach aches
at the thought of Max reporting my actions back to his dad,
then feeding information to their attorney. Sending Max a
message was the right thing, the only thing, to do.

I punch a playlist titled "Happy Shit" with my gloved finger and amp up the volume as loud as my cars will tolerate
joy. What I'd give for a video of Max tipping over backward

into the snow. I'd turn it into a GIF and hit replay a million times. Caption reading: *I'm Max. Ex-girlfriend stalker. Oh, no! Shit! Oops! Splat.*

A lady next to me at the red light stares in my direction, her eyebrows scrunched and full of worry. I salute her. She has a sticker on the rear passenger-side window advertising her perfect stick-figure family complete with one dog and one cat. Animals who probably share the same pet bed. I roll my window down and shout, "That sticker belongs on the back!"

Her window cracks an inch. "What?"

"Your stick-figure art! It goes on the back of your SUV, not the side window!"

She scowls and swats her hand. I crank my music and laugh, flashing a toothy grin while slamming the gas pedal as the light shifts to green. My tires squeal.

Max, head to toe in his black running gear. What was he thinking stalking me in the snow? Even his black hair was recognizable. I sigh, shuffle the songs. The heater blasts as a slow, piano-heavy ballad starts, and my thoughts turn to Max's face. His nose and cheeks pink from the cold air. Chin and cheekbones I used to frame with the palms of my hands and watch as his eyes searched for answers somewhere deep inside me. We could stare at each other for minutes without speaking. His dark eyes, seeking secrets I hadn't shared, not stopping until he understood them. I mute the music and push back into my seat.

At Cal's funeral, Max stopped seeking my eyes. At the

cemetery, he quit looking at me altogether. Now Max searches for me, but he's not hunting for my eyes or my heart anymore. He has to be fact-finding, following his dad's orders, doing what he's told. Dad warned me to stay away from Max. He said, "He's just like his father—out to hurt us." Maybe Dad's right and Max is gathering information that will help his family win their wrongful death case against us. Would Max really do that? It seems out of character for Max. But I don't know him anymore.

My head hurts thinking about Dad and Max. I'm sandwiched between them. Nothing makes sense anymore. My dad hasn't thought clearly since the accident. Every day he changes into someone I don't recognize, and as hard as I try to muffle his words, they penetrate and hook me. Dad has become a wrecking ball that swings at me, at Mom, at Grace, and no matter how quickly we duck and dive, it's breaking off hunks of who we once were. One more swing and I'll be nothing but debris.

And Max. The guy I once loved. Now a pawn sent to follow Aggi. Find Aggi. Keep a watchful eye on Aggi. *Is that what you're doing, Max?*

When I trace his steps, how he runs where I work, eats bagels where I eat muffins, slurps coffee where I sip tea, it's obvious. Ever since Max's family attorney sent a stack of papers the size of a small mountain, Max pops up unannounced.

My father insists Max's mission is to find something on me that will help his family win their case. Max's parents blame

63

Kate for killing Cal, and my parents blame Max's family for killing Kate. Dad says, "Guilt kills quicker than a gun." Though Dad's words confuse me. Kate was suffering, as we all were. Max's parents had lost their oldest son and they were grieving. Everything happened so fast. Cal was here and then gone in seconds.

Kate didn't know the storm was whirling their way. She didn't know she'd hit sheets of black ice and skid down a ravine. She had no idea the car would roll three times and she'd live with the pain and guilt of killing her best friend while walking away bruise-free. My sister did not kill herself. Suffering ended her life. We ignored her cries for help. We lost sight of her as we mourned for Cal. Then the hushed voices at night in the kitchen turned to shouts in the driveway. Our fathers, preoccupied with pain and anger, even revenge. If I could rewind the clock, crawl into bed with my sister, wrap her in my arms, and tell her nothing was her fault, I would. I should have warned her about the ice storm. I had tinkered with the weather station earlier in the day but was still learning what the readings meant. Had I known what I know now about weather and predictability, I might have been able to save Cal and Kate.

But Max had met me on the roof of the science building, and within minutes we were laughing and kissing, ripping off each other's clothes. There was a goddamn weather station with alerts and indicators warning that Kate shouldn't drive, but all I cared about was telling Max how hot I was getting by

64

the furnace—a convenient excuse to take off my shirt, bra, pants. Had I checked my phone messages. Had I checked the weather station. Had I called my dad and demanded he pick Kate and Cal up from the concert or make them stay in a hotel overnight instead of driving sixty miles home in the dark while the sky shot needles of ice. I should have stopped Kate from driving.

I roll down my car window and tilt my head into the wind. There is not enough air in this world for me to catch my breath. My head pounds, and I pull over at the last cross-road before reaching the narrow pine-lined road toward the lake. I snatch my phone from my purse and frantically type a message to Kate: *How do I make them understand it wasn't anyone's fault?* But even as I type, the guilt cloud hovers.

As I sink into the seat, my eyes close, and I draw deep breaths. In my head, a ping sounds. Kate, texting me back. I tap the phone screen and imagine her message. *Everyone's processing things the only way they know how. Doesn't make it right, I know, but please be patient.*

I press my forehead against the glass as gears grind behind me. My eyes pop open as Max bulldozes around the turn, gray slush slopping against the side of my car. His brakes tap three times, and the Jeep fishtails. He must have seen me. Will he stop? I sit up in my seat, wondering how close Max will get before we're both caught. I wonder if he ever feels like risking it all.

10

MAX

I SWERVE TO AVOID HITTING Aggi's car. Did she break down? Should I stop and make sure she's okay? But I can't. It's against the rules. The lawsuit. Whatever you want to call that damn *order* that's ruining our lives.

After the episode in the parking lot, I'm unsure what Aggi might do if I turn around and ask if she needs assistance. Throw a snowball at my face? I gear the Jeep down. She probably pulled over to talk to Umé. Besides, Aggi's lived in these woods since she was a kid. She's more aware of safety and survival than me. But what if her tire was flat? I rack my brain trying to remember if I've ever seen Aggi change a tire. I feel it's something about her I'd remember. Did her tire look flat? Did I even look at her tires? *Shit*. What if she's out of gas?

I'll call Umé. If something's wrong with Aggi, Umé will know. My fingers hover over the phone screen. The last time I asked Umé about Aggi, she warned me to leave Aggi alone or her father would blast me into the afterlife with my brother. She almost made me cry. Umé can be alarmingly blunt, especially where her duties as Aggi's protector are concerned. But she is Aggi's best friend, and I've known and loved her like a sister my entire life.

My phone vibrates in my hand, and Henry's name lights up.

"Can you call Aggi?" I shout into the phone.

"Hello to you, too," Henry says in complete monotone.

My words fly. "Seriously, Henry. I just passed her car on the side of the road. She might need help. Can you call her? Will you call her? You know I can't call her."

Henry huffs. I possibly detect a moan, but then he says, "Yeah. Sure. But then I'm calling you right back. Important stuff to discuss, so be ready."

Henry hangs up as I'm turning onto the road to the lake. I slow down and glance in my rearview mirror, wishing Aggi would appear behind me so I know for sure she's okay.

Aggi and I used to race each other home from school when we weren't riding in the same car. As soon as I'd turn onto the road leading to the lake, she'd be right on my tail. I'd ease up on the gas, act like I was reaching for something on the seat or dash, and let her whiz around me while she shouted from her window, "I win!" I grin just thinking about the happiness on her face. I'd jump naked in the lake, get chased by a wild turkey, or collapse face-first in the snow if it meant Aggi would smile like that again.

My phone beeps as I'm circling the driveway we share with the Franks.

I slam the Jeep into park. "Is she okay?" I shout into the phone.

"She's fine." Henry's using his dad voice. "Nothing's wrong. Relax, Max. Aggi's fine."

"Is that what she said?" My voice has become that of a worried grandmother.

"*I* said it, Max."

"But you talked to her? You heard her voice? What'd she sound like?"

"All good. No worries. Like I said, Aggi's fine."

I exhale. "Thanks, buddy."

"Now, about this evening." Henry leans on his survival skills—like abrupt topic changes—that hold us together as friends even after Aggi and I stopped seeing each other. Okay, after Aggi and I just stopped. For the record, we never broke up. At my brother's funeral, I had a difficult time looking anywhere beyond my feet. Aggi tried to talk to me, but I distanced myself. I regret those actions now. Had I let her take my hand when she reached for it, things might be different. But I'd heard words—like "wrongful death"—my dad murmured to my mom, and everything began spinning out of control. But even then, I believe—eventually—I'd have found my way back to Aggi if her father had not threatened me.

That night on the roof of the science building, as our hands found each other's bodies, our love felt eternal. I fight to remember the feelings I had right before the calls came. But guilt fights, too, and is much stronger than me. Maybe Aggi and I would have survived if we hadn't been having sex the moment my brother was killed. Maybe Kate and Cal would be alive if Aggi and I had never been together.

"This evening?" I repeat back to Henry.

"Join me at Connor's. Lake-kid party. That's what Connor called it."

A groan unleashes. I'm not big on parties, especially those thrown by Connor.

Surprisingly, Henry wants to go. Since I've known Henry, he's tried desperately to change his image, what people think about him and where he's from the backwoods of North Carolina—so a party with lake kids doesn't exactly suit him. Of course, it depends which side of the lake we're talking about.

But then the possibility hits me. "Do you know who's going to be there?" I force myself to sound less eager, more non-chalant. If Henry picks up on an inflection, he'll assume I'm hoping Aggi will be there, which is spot-on.

"Everyone," Henry says. "Connor invited the entire lake."

My initial reaction was to decline the invite, but now I'm intrigued by the likelihood of Aggi being there. Perhaps Aggi waved when I passed her on the side of the road. There were seconds when my eyes were somewhere other than my rearview mirror, and seconds are all it takes to miss a wave. I mean, she totally could have lifted her hand and I didn't see. It would be plain rude of me not to go to Connor's party and at least present a second chance at a wave.

Henry clears his throat.

"What time?" I ask, again with the nonchalant monotone.

"I'll find out and call you back," Henry says. "But remember to bring a swimsuit and towel."

"No way! Connor's polar-bear plunges are fucking ridiculous."

Henry laughs. "Hot-tubbing. No one in their right mind's going into that lake. It's supposed to snow tonight."

I chuckle, nervously.

"So I'll call you back. I want to see if Connor invited any girls from town. Wouldn't it be wonderful if a girl who wasn't from Walabash Woods showed?"

We pause, my rebuttal forming on my tongue.

"Don't answer that," Henry snaps. "But I'm hopeful, Max. Someday my Brienne of Tarth is going to ride in on a beautiful Lipizzan horse and scoop me up in her arms." Henry stops himself. "Okay, so I'll call you back."

"I'll be here waiting, Sir Lannister."

Henry's burned bridges with most of the lake girls. Technically, there are only seven lake girls around our age, including Aggi, and they all think of Henry as the dreaded friend. The one to count on, not date. Henry's also seen as trouble, not boyfriend material, thanks to his deep-seated prison roots.

Families living around Plum Lake believe a certain thing about Henry, but none of them know him like I do.

Henry, or Hank, as his dad slapped on his birth certificate, comes from a long line of convicts. Henry's dad insists he's next in line to commit a crime that'll reunite him with his oldest brother behind bars. He says it like it's a badge of honor. Henry's brothers and father expect Henry's path to follow theirs, but they don't know the Henry I do. They see poor, white-trash Hank. They don't see Heart-of-Gold Henry, as Aggi always called him.

Henry is the guy you call when your truck's stuck in the snow. The friend you talk to when your heart breaks into pieces. The one you confide life's secrets to.

I once thought the perfect girl for Henry was Umé. She's one of the few people who push him to do better, be better, or at least help convince him he's something other than his family thinks he should be. But Umé's not into Henry. She says a guy's got to do a lot to impress her, and as of now she's quite happy dating a townie girl she met at a gas station. Not that there's anything wrong with meeting someone at a gas station; it's just not the place I think of as a nice backdrop for a revisit on your one-year dating anniversary. Of course, who am I to judge? Aggi and me on top of the science building might be even more ridiculous. But what I wouldn't give to be holding Aggi while we stare at the stars on top of that roof.

Umé lives near Connor on the other side of the lake, except Connor's property spreads and sprawls across ten acres and

71

includes a restored mill–turned–livable space. Technically, Umé is Connor's neighbor, but the pines obstruct their view. In actuality, Connor's neighbors are trees and deer, eagles and rock. Connor's parents have all the land their money could buy.

The lake presents a mix of classes. Only one Connor and many Henrys.

When I say my family lives on a lake, transplants from the north assume a large lake house or three-story cabin with A-framed balconies, not shared property with communal drives. People don't understand the difference between those living on the north side of Plum Lake and those on the south side, unless, of course, you're from Plum Lake. In fact, if you look at the southeast side of the lake, you won't have to look far to find two single-wide trailers with tires on the roofs and a Porta-Potty blanketed with Christmas lights. One of the trailers is owned by Henry's dad, and I use the term "owned" loosely, as Henry's dad and twin brothers stole it from a construction site and spray-painted the logo into a large black blob. Now it serves as a second bathroom on their junkyard estate.

On our property, the land we share with the Franks, lake living is a comfortable remodeled rancher with added-on bonus room and screened-in back porch. Inside, we're updated and modern and very middle class. Right now, though, we're lower than middle class, with the lingering funeral and legal bills. The refrigeration company my dad owned with Aggi's father is suffering, too, since Mr. Frank quit showing up for work. Our fathers built the business together when they graduated high school. My dad took classes at a community college, learned the trade, and taught Aggi's dad how to tinker with refrigeration units and air conditioners. They did everything together. Work, boat, fish. Now all they do is blame.

Connor lives on the opposite side of the lake from Aggi and me. His nineteenth-century home is the real deal. Really restored, really expensive. Connor's parents moved here from Silicon Valley a few years ago and brought the hipster with them. Connor wears stop-sign-red pants and tailored seersucker blazers complete with matching pocket squares. He folds the square point to match his mood. Why do I know so much about Connor's fashion? He tells everyone. He says, "The one-point-triangle pocket square means today I'm on point—ambitious, precise, going places." Connor has confidence I wish I had. He has a burgeoning beard, too, but it's a rumored fact that Connor's dad had beard implants to make his face look like a Chia Pet. Connor says if his own whiskers don't fill in the way he likes, he'll add the same implants. Have I mentioned on most days I refer to Connor as an asshole?

Connor could be tolerable in small doses. I have nothing against his pants or pocket squares, but he morphed quickly into full-fledged ass at Kate's funeral, when he wrapped his arms around Aggi and told her he was there for her, day or night. His affections for Aggi are as fake as his father's beard, and lately, whenever I'm around him, whenever my heart

73

punches at my chest and tries to convince me that what I'm doing will eventually matter, Connor's affections for Aggi grow loud and elephant-like. He knows about our families' falling-out, and I swear, he loves it more than he loves his pocket square.

Henry insists Connor is only trying to fit in like the rest of us, but Henry's an eternal optimist, and I have become mostly negative.

After I've worried myself into a state of despair thinking about Connor and Aggi holding hands, her tugging at his pocket square while he chuckles and nods, Henry calls back.

"Pick you up at four. Remember, swimsuit and towel. Don't forget."

"I changed my mind. I'm not going."

Henry exhales.

"It's just that . . . I don't think . . . Ouch!"

"What's wrong?"

I glance at my chin in the bathroom mirror and smear on a thin veil of Neosporin. "I scraped my face exercising earlier and it looks ridiculous."

Henry scoffs. "Well, thankfully it's not a zit on your nose."

"What's that mean?"

"Just slap on some antibiotic cream and wait for me."

Henry hangs up before I can argue.

Henry's on my porch at four o'clock and we're piling into my Jeep and driving to Connor's lake house for hot-tubbing. I've forgotten my towel.

"So I decided to hide my brothers' truck keys," Henry says, flicking pebbles of snow from the cuffs of his pants onto the floorboard of my Jeep.

The fresh cut and purple bruise on the bridge of Henry's nose worry me, but I decide not to mention them, as I'm certain the damage to his face has everything to do with the reason Henry hid his brothers' keys. After witnessing several eyebrow gashes and black eyes, I've learned to give Henry space to share details of his horrible home life when he's ready. Henry sniffs, twitching his nose like a rabbit, and I motion toward the glove box so he can save face. "Tissues in there. I'm catching that same damn cold."

Henry tilts his head in my direction and half smiles. Our eyes meet, and I nod until Henry reciprocates. He's helped me save face too many times to count, but he knows I'm here, ready to talk, when he is.

After a long pause, Henry reaches into his coat pocket. "When I said I hid my brothers' keys, I meant . . ." He jingles the ring of keys in the air.

I slap the steering wheel. "You stole them."

Henry shrugs. "You know how they get when they drink. They wanted to wrestle me, and the more they drank the rougher they got. I could have beaten the shit out of them, but you know I don't operate like that. Instead, I did them a favor. Waited until they passed out and likely saved their damn lives." Henry tucks his arms behind his head.

"What a great brother you are," I say sarcastically. "So

great, in fact, that you're going to get your ass kicked—that is if you actually make it through the night!"

"No reason to be scared, Maxwell."

I shiver. The twins are nothing like Henry. Sometimes I wonder how Henry could possibly be related to any of his family members, especially his twin brothers. "Don't they have a second set of keys?"

Henry rubs his knuckle along the bump on his nose and winces. "Yeah, well, I may have taken those, too. No one at my house was in any condition to drive but me."

"You're scaring me."

Henry slaps the dash, a grin spreading across his face. "Oh, Max! They're going to be so pissed. I just hope they don't remember my dad also has a set of keys."

11

MAX

"WAIT ON THE GRAND STAIRCASE," Connor says at the door, and rushes up the stairs.

"Grand what?" I shoot Henry a *What the hell?* look as we walk inside Connor's house.

Henry shrugs and drapes his large body across the bottom steps of the Grand Staircase while we wait for Connor to dip his body in cologne.

Henry tucks his knees to his chest, cradles his long legs. Connor's going to be a while, so I plop into a fuzzy black chair and sink deep into the cushions. My legs ache from this morning's half run, half jog, full fall. My mind races over the repercussions of Aggi seeing me, but I'm also enjoying the possibility that she saw me and spun out on purpose. At least then I'd know she cared enough to sling slush at my face. Better than being invisible.

I rub my forehead and sigh as Henry's always-a-good-friend radar flips on.

"Tonight will be good for you," he says. "Get you out and around other people. Away from She Who Must Not Be Named."

I moan. "Aggi?"

"Is that her name?" Henry locks his eyes on the floor and scuffs his foot across the tile. "We need to resuscitate life back into you. Tonight is rich with oxygen. The trees pulse. I feel it."

My mouth gapes as I'm about to ask Henry to elaborate on how exactly the trees pulse when the sharp piney smell of cologne jabs my nose.

"Fuckers!" Connor shouts.

I groan and Henry pushes off the banister, shooting me a look that says, *Play nice.*

For Henry's sake, I ignore Connor's annoying salutation, but his pants? Impossible to overlook.

"Nice yellow pants," I mumble, and Connor pats his front pockets.

"You like 'em, huh? Had 'em sent over from Melrose Ave—"

I cut him off. "I didn't say I liked—"

Henry jumps between us. "So who's coming over tonight?"

Connor turns toward Henry. "Lake crew. A few townies."

"Lake crew?" I repeat. "You mean, lake kids?"

Connor's eyebrows lift, and his eyes dart from my head to my toes and back again. "How's Aggi?" He grins and we're suddenly back on the staircase where he called us "fuckers."

My face freezes, eyes squint. The temperature in the room rises as my hands form fists.

Henry glances at my hands and shakes his head. I exhale and fall into a wing-back chair. Connor rolls his eyes, and I squeeze the back of my neck, stare at the floor, and wait for him to answer his own question, offering a full report on exactly how Aggi is.

On cue, Connor says, "I texted her last night." He digs into his pocket and pulls out his phone. His fingers race across the screen as he swipes for content. "Aggi said she was doing well, great actually, and asked me to come over. Bitch is ripe."

I lunge from the chair, and Henry straight-arms my chest. Connor steps back with hands raised. "Jesus, Maxwell! Settle down! Thought you were long over her."

I swat Henry's arm aside and grab Connor's checked shirt collar with both hands. "Don't ever refer to Aggi as a bitch! Do you hear me? In fact, don't refer to her at all. Don't even say her name."

Connor squirms. His voice a squeal. "Put me down!"

It takes a second to register that Connor's toes are scratching at the ground like one of his family's free-range chickens.

My cheeks burn. I need to dip my face in snow. When I drop Connor and straighten his collar, his furrowed brow and worried eyes scare me.

"What the hell's wrong with you?" Connor shouts. "I invite you into my home and you act like this?"

Henry slides between us, patting at my chest. "Relax, buddy. Let it go."

"But he called her—"

Henry whispers, "He's a pig. His words, irrelevant."

"But—"

"Let it go, Max. Let her go. Don't you think it's time?"

I ponder Henry's words. Time is all I think about. How I'm running out of it. Every day I wake up, still here, still breathing, yet given another chance to let it go or make it right. To be brave, to fight for love, to chase after what I want. But I'm failing miserably. Scared as hell. Time, so finite. A limited commodity. And it's never on my side.

I shrug, staring blankly at Henry. I'm changing. I'm angry. If Henry and I were alone, I'd confess these things. That I'm so afraid of becoming passive like my parents that I'm becoming as angry as Aggi's dad. I need time, but the clock won't stop ticking. I have to talk to Aggi, but not in front of Connor's lemon-drop pants and piney cologne.

I spin around at the door. "Going home."

"What about the party?" Henry asks, and there's softness in his voice. A sound that always catches me off guard, especially when I'm fighting hard to stay mad at the circumstances of my life. Henry has an ability to stay calm in the middle of a storm.

"Let him go," Connor snaps.

I pause with my hand on the doorknob. Voices mix, whirl, twist into the shape of a tornado. *Go to her, Max. If you want her, you have to go after her.* Then the wind changes direction, and I hear his hate-filled words. *Stay away from my daughter. If it weren't for you . . .*

I slam the door so hard a porch planter topples over, cracks, and dumps dirt. I skid my foot through the soil and shout at the sky, "Cal! Do you hear me? What the fuck do I do now?"

12

UMÉ TEXTS AND ASKS IF I'm going to the bonfire near East Lake cabins. She says everyone's meeting at Connor's, heading to the dock, and hot-tubbing afterward. I send Umé a picture of a pervy-looking guy with a molester-style mustache and thin-rimmed glasses floating upright in a Jacuzzi full of girls. Then follow with a cartoon character barfing. Umé's no stranger to my feelings about Connor. He's pushy, flashy, rich. The exact opposite of what I'm used to. Connor wants to fit in with the lake kids, but he goes about it the wrong way.

My phone buzzes and flashes Umé's name.

"Pictures didn't answer your question?"

"Yeah. Tell me how you really feel. But seriously, I'm getting you out of the house before it swallows your soul."

"And Connor's supposed to save me?"

Umé snorts. "Jesus George Michael Christ! You will save yourself. With my help, of course."

"But Dr. Nelson's going to bring Grace home this afternoon, and I can't leave her alone with my mom and dad."

"So bring her along."

Umé, my reasonable and persuasive friend. I wish I could be there for her like she is for me, but Umé never needs me the way I need her. Sometimes, after we've spent the day together, and she's listened to me talk about Kate and Max and everyone I've lost, I go home, crawl into my bed, and imagine myself as a tornado sucking up everything in its path. I spin and uproot trees, suck up lawn chairs and mailboxes. I am the cause of so much destruction. I am the suck zone.

"So?"

"Not this afternoon. I'm sorry. I would be horrible company."

But Umé refuses to listen, and within thirty minutes, she stands on my porch, eyes darting around the living room. "Is Grace here yet?"

I motion toward the driveway as Dr. Nelson pulls alongside the house and Grace bounds from the car.

"Hey, Gracie!"

Grace waves at Umé and races inside the house, tearing her coat from her thin limbs and tossing it over a chair.

"Mom and Dad are upstairs," I call after her, but she's on the couch, feet kicking a dust-covered caulking gun across the coffee table, and flipping channels with the remote.

Dr. Nelson taps the horn, and I wave, then plop down on the couch beside Grace. Her eyes stick to the screen filled with talking animals.

"Have you and Grace eaten dinner?" Umé asks. "'Cause I'm starved."

"Dr. Nelson made me eat before I left, but I can always eat again," Grace says without eye contact.

I rest my hand on Grace's shoulder, and she scoots away from me, tucking herself into the corner of the couch.

"If you're hungry, I can make us dinner," I say, but Grace refuses to look at me.

I think about the last meal I prepared for Grace. A can of minestrone soup, lukewarm, and in a water glass because the soup bowls and cups sat dirty in the dishwasher. All that murky broth turns my stomach.

"Nobody's making anything to eat," Umé says, tightening her scarf. "Grab your coats, kids—we're going out for dinner."

The three of us end up at our only option within a twenty-mile driving radius if we don't want pizza from Lucio & Sons. Plum Lake Café. Complete with a giant plum painted on the side of a weather-stained building. The dark wood and purple paint make the plum look like an oversized blueberry.

Becky, the blue-eyeshadowed waitress, slaps the swinging door to the kitchen and shouts, "Be right there! Sit anywhere you like!"

The restaurant is empty, customary during the winter season, so we sit in a purple, padded, crescent-moon-shaped booth designed for six customers.

"I am starving," Umé says, tearing open a sugar packet and pouring it into her mouth.

"Me too." I glance at Grace. She tucks two napkins into the waistband of her black ruffled skirt and yanks at the knees of her tights.

Umé drops a fist on the table. "When's the last time your mom or dad went to the grocery store?"

I shake my head and motion toward Grace, shooting Umé the *not now* eyes.

Grace squints at me, then Umé.

"What?" Umé asks.

"Not long ago."

Grace grunts. "Why do you make excuses for them?"

I open my mouth, close, open again. "We have food in the house. We have . . . soup."

"Thanks to Dr. Nelson," Grace mumbles.

True, but Grace shouldn't be aware the cupboards are spotty or the food in the refrigerator requires a sniff test before tasting.

"We need to get you out of the house more," Umé says, running her fingers along the sugar packets. "With all due respect, Aggi, your parents need help. Family members? A therapist?"

Grace drops her chin and pushes against the seat.

Umé has lived my last year alongside me, as tragic as it's been, and she knows my survival skills. How I can't stand to be out of my room for more than a few minutes. My three-ingredient rule. And what makes Umé the best friend anyone could ask for is that she never judges me or my parents, even behind the sarcastic tone and raised eyebrows. She gets seriously irritated with my folks, though she'd never admit it.

Becky appears at our table without menus or a writing utensil. Umé shouts out our order. "Three platters of sweet potato fries smothered in cheddar. Three cheddar-and-chicken biscuits. And two fried green tomatoes. Grace?" Grace nods.

"Make that three tomatoes," Umé continues. "And one order of chicken tenders." She winks at Grace, and Grace grins.

I'm salivating as Becky mentally notes the food list. "Dipping sauce for the tenders?"

"Ranch, please," I say, and Grace gasps.

"Do you still have the Brie and Carolina hot sauce?" she asks Becky.

"Sure do, little friend." Becky clicks her tongue. "Drinks?"

"All the pop," Umé says, slapping the table. The silverware clanks.

"And hot tea for me, please," Grace says. "With honey."

Becky nods and rushes toward the kitchen shouting, "Wake up, Gill! Order in and these kids are hungry!"

"You *are* hungry," I say, tucking a foot beneath my butt.

"Always," Umé says. "And somebody needs to make sure you eat."

"I'm eating just fine." Grace unzips her coat and slips her arms out of the sleeves. "Thanks to Dr. Nelson's peach and meat pies."

86

Becky drops off three dark and three pink sodas. All the pop.

"Hot tea on its way."

"Thanks, Becky," we say in unison, and she hesitates at the table, circling her rag in the same spot.

I draw a deep breath and prepare for what's coming.

"Saw your daddy in here yesterday, Aggi Mae. He doesn't look so well."

My natural reaction is to stick up for my father. Tell Becky that Dad's doing the best he can, which isn't much and that makes me angry, but I nod and wait for her next question. Becky smiles as if she knows exactly what I'm going through. Maybe her daddy was like mine. A father who copes with grief by yanking at the loose strings barely holding his family together until we're a tangled pile of thread. A father who won't look his two living children in their eyes because he's too busy shouting, pointing fingers, and blaming others for an accident. I think about Umé's words. How my parents do need help, and if Dad doesn't seek it out he's going to combust.

Umé studies me, lifts her glass without breaking her gaze, and fishes for her straw with her tongue. She slurps until the glass is empty, shoves it at Becky, saying, "Going to need a refill. I am *so* thirsty."

Umé, protecting me from questions I don't have answers for.

But Becky pauses, and storm clouds swirl in my head. Even if Becky's questions originate from a caring heart, they will push me to a place I don't want to go.

"How's your mama doing? Saw her walking near the college the other day. I waved, called her name, but she wouldn't look up from her feet. She didn't look okay. Is she all right?"

I close my eyes, and Umé clears her throat. "Soda? Becky, please." Umé's voice sounds like her mother's after her daughter's arrived home fifteen minutes past curfew.

Becky spins on her heel, taking Umé's hint, and scurries off toward the soda machine.

"You have to know how to handle these nosy villagers."

I push a smile. "Low energy, remember?"

"No energy's more like it. Drink up." Umé pushes a soda at me. "Fill your blood with sugar."

The three of us slurp in silence until Umé dabs a napkin to her lips and says, "Something interesting happened today." She double-clicks her phone. "Henry texted me and asked what you were doing earlier on the side of the road."

I straighten in my seat, dropping my foot to the floor.

"He said Max saw you and got worried." Umé brushes her fingers over her phone screen and, with her head down, looks up only with her eyes. She whispers, "Should we believe him?"

I exhale as I do when the conversation shifts to Max. "Henry? Definitely. When have you ever known Henry to lie?"

Umé forcefully shakes her head. "Not Henry. Max."

I hold a breath.

Umé nudges me with her eyebrows.

"He's following me again."

88

"You saw him at work?"

Grace moans. "Max loves you. What else do you expect him to do?"

We stare at Grace, my mouth gaping, as Becky reappears at the table and slides platters of smothered fries in front of our faces. I grab two cheeseless sticks from the edge of the plate while Umé tears open a packet of Lactaid and dumps the pill into her mouth.

"Thanks, Becky."

Becky hesitates, and for a moment I think she's going to unload more questions on me, but when Umé shoves another empty glass at her, Becky beelines toward the counter.

Umé wiggles a fry in her hand like a wand. "Please tell me Max isn't planning to do something ridiculous."

I chuckle. "This is Max we're talking about."

Umé frowns. "I'm not sure how I feel about Max following you to work. The whole tragedy is awful. But these fries." A fake British accent ensues. "Oh, bloody hell, these fries are scrummy."

I laugh, thankful for Umé and how she reminds me that I'm a whole person, three-dimensional, who has not lost the two critical pieces holding me together, upright and in place. Umé helps lessen the guilt I cling to over losing Kate. She helps me think of Max without blame. The contempt my father feels toward Max and his family has nothing to do with me. If only Dad understood this.

When Kate died, Umé told me to let every emotion have

its time. Anger. Hurt. Guilt. I went numb while Umé shook my shoulders and begged for one tear to squeeze from the corner of my eye and spill onto my cheek. Something held my throat, tight at first, and I could barely breathe. Minutes felt like hours. Hours like days. Time stopped after the accident. My motion froze with fear. How do I go on without her? How do I live without my sister?

It was midnight on a Friday when I called Umé and begged her to come over. She arrived within minutes and stood on my porch wrapped in pink cat-printed pajamas and a terry bathrobe for a coat. I felt the dam of salty tears and snot building, pushing, ready to burst, and as soon as Umé draped her arms across my shoulders, it broke.

"Talk to me like I'm Kate," Umé said. "Tell me . . . her . . . everything you need to say. Everything you've been holding inside."

The only words that formed were questions. "What could we have done? What should we have done? Why weren't we enough? Why weren't you?"

Umé never answered the questions I whispered to Kate. I only needed her to absorb them like a sponge. We've never revisited that moment on the porch, but I know Umé's holding my questions safe, protecting them from stupid truths, and when I'm ready, she won't have to answer.

After we devour our chicken biscuits, fries, and green tomatoes, and Grace spoons the remaining dipping sauce into her mouth, we drive toward the lake and Connor's supersized log cabin, belting out songs from Umé's playlist. Being away from the house, free of worry that Mom and Dad might say something that will cause Grace pain, feels like an oxygen mask strapped to my face. Whether it's the cold air or the ease of being with my best friend, I am resuscitated. And with Grace beside me, where Mom and Dad won't hurt her with their words, distant stares, and folded arms, I can breathe.

We pull onto the narrow, private pine-lined drive leading up to Connor's cabin. After Umé parks, she drums the steering wheel and says, "I have an announcement to make."

Grace squeezes between the front seats, grabbing our shoulders. Her cold hand slides against the base of my neck and a tingle shoots down my arm. Grace hasn't touched me in months. I miss her and she's right beside me.

"We're all ears," Grace says, and I smile.

Umé tilts her head, and I nod for her to go ahead, proceed with caution in front of the ten-going-on-sixty-year-old.

"I broke up with that girl from town." Umé exhales and slams her back against her seat. "God, that felt good to say!"

I moan. "No. Oh, no. You were perfect for each—"

"Nope!" Umé pushes her palm in my face. "She was not perfect. She deserved a good dumping."

"Seriously? But I thought she was the one—"

"The one? Are you serious? Let me tell you what *the one* was capable of." Umé clears her throat. "Last week, we're driving back to my house and I shout, 'Stop! There's a squirrel!' and do you know what that human being with no soul did?"

I shake my head, and Grace clutches her chest.

"She stepped on the fucking gas!"

"No!" Grace gasps, and Umé clutches Grace's hand.

"She did. She fucking did."

I wince and Umé catches herself. "Sorry, Grace. Don't repeat my words to your parents."

"Is the squirrel okay?" Grace asks.

"Oh, yeah, she didn't run it over. Those squirrels are nearly impossible to hit. But the way she laughed about it sent a chill up my spine. Like what kind of monster is this girl? Like what else is she hiding in her basement?"

Grace and I nod, unsure where to steer the conversation.

"You'd think she was related to the Beacon boys," Umé says. "Didn't Henry's brothers pay a huge fine a while back for killing a cat? I have heard those rumors and believe them all."

"Well, as long as you're happy," I say.

"I'm ecstatic! I mean, it does suck a little that she had to do something like that, but better to see her true nature now than later. Besides, she wasn't ready for me."

I smile, knowing exactly what Umé means. I never met her girlfriend from town, the one Umé raved about for months—claiming she was the one—but I'm certain she wasn't ready for Umé. The world does not deserve Umé yet, but maybe it will someday, and when it does, watch out.

Umé unbuckles her seat belt. "Let's go have some fun."

Grace climbs out of the car but I freeze, unable to move.

I scan the driveway for Max's Jeep. What if he's here? Umé walks to the passenger side and opens my door.

"What's wrong?"

I exhale and crane my neck behind me. "Think he's here?"

Umé shrugs. "So what if he is?" A smile pushes, but like a glitch, it disappears, leaving concerned eyes. Umé knows as well as I do what will happen if Max and I show up at the same party. We talk or we don't talk, but either way, shit will always find its way back to my dad. This town is too small to be safe.

Umé extends a hand, and I clamp onto her fingers. On the way to the stone steps, Grace tugs the back of my coat and I slip out of Umé's grip.

"Please don't treat me like your little sister tonight." Grace scrunches her brow, demanding a serious response. "I mean it, Aggi. Treat me like you would a friend."

I nibble my lip and promise Grace, though I wish she would let me knuckle the top of her head, clutch her in my arms, and rock her like a baby. Grace has pushed my cuddles away since Kate died. It sounds cliché, but a part of Grace died with Kate. The part that giggled when a ladybug landed on her fingertip, the part that etched her name in snow with a stick and marveled at the loopy letters, the part that sniffed her fuzzy blanket until she fell asleep while I grazed her eyebrows with the back of my nail. Grace aged ten years in five days, and I'm not sure I will ever get my little sister back. The sister I want to hug and hold and tickle and squeeze.

At Connor's door, Henry greets us like he owns the place. My built-in invader alert goes off, because where Henry is, Max lurks. Shooting my head to one side, then the other, I spin around until Henry reaches toward me and says, "Relax, Aggi. He's not here. He went home a while ago."

"That's right." Connor slides into the foyer in fuzzy socks and blinds us with his sunshine pants. He attempts to scoop my hand with his, but I stuff my fingers into my purse and dig for something. Pepper spray, perhaps. "Max went home, where he belongs," Connor continues. "No babies allowed." He lifts an eyebrow in Grace's direction.

Grace glares.

"Who said anything about Max?" *Max*. His name is beginning to sound foreign. That's what happens when you're afraid to speak it. Like goddamn Voldemort. "I never said anything about him. Max. Maxwell. Maxwell Granger." There. His name sounds perfectly familiar now.

Umé's eyes smile, and Henry folds his arms. They watch me with sympathetic eyes, afraid they've said too much or not enough, until Connor clears his throat. "Help me light the fire?"

Connor's backyard is more an extension of the woods— a few man-made clearings packed with slate and rubbery bushes—but the overgrown grass and pine-straw-covered ground spread out to the edge of the lake. Connor grabs a flashlight and leads us down a snow-and-dirt-covered path to the dock.

I reach for Grace's hand out of instinct and she pushes it away as a reminder that my little sister can handle herself.

We reach a pebbled trail lined with bamboo tiki torches. Connor stops at the first torch, slips his backpack off his shoulders, and retrieves a long BBQ lighter. He zigzags from torch to torch, lighting the wicks and shouting, "Poof!" after each flame ignites. There are five million torches, which cue Umé's annoyance.

"Beckoning an aircraft carrier, are we?" Umé kicks a mound of icy snow. "Or maybe the mother ship? Because I'm not sure you have enough damn torches and it's not quite dark yet."

"Keeping mosquitoes at bay," Connor says. "Candles are made of citronella. Your ass will thank me later." He winks at Umé, and she winks back with her middle finger.

"Too cold for mosquitoes, California boy."

Adirondack chairs circle a rocky fire pit surrounded by more torches. Umé plops down in the only recliner and says, "Where are all the women you claimed would be here waiting for us?"

Connor whips around to face me, and my skin prickles as if a thousand mosquitoes alit and bit in unison. "You and Aggi are here." He grins. "The rest will surely follow."

Doubtful. Connor has money that buys craft beer and tiki torches but doesn't always buy friends. At least not lake-kid friends. We're different from the friends Connor claims to have left in California. Most of the lake kids Connor begs to build friendships with work jobs so they can buy heat and groceries for their families, not lemon-drop pants or next season's leather-yoke shirt jackets from Barneys. No one blames Connor for his wealth, no one's jealous of his dipped-and-dyed good looks—the kids on the lake just don't understand excess and the freedom it brings.

Within a couple of minutes, voices wind down the torch-lit trail. Umé smiles, and I snag a chair next to her. Grace meanders toward the lake and sits on the dock by herself with legs dangling over the side. Light from the torches shines a halo over her head as she tosses rocks into the black water, which is becoming an oil slick under the moonlit sky. A thin sheet of ice near the shore has broken into three pieces and floats back and forth as Grace aims and throws rocks into the water. Once in a while, Grace's pebble connects with the ice and splinters it into fragments that disappear in the lake.

I run through a checklist of Grace's clothing in my head. The items designed to keep her warm and safe. Fuzzy coat, furry scarf, waterproof boots. No gloves. "Grace!" I shout. "Your gloves! They're in your coat pocket!"

"Not your kid sister tonight!" Grace shouts back, reminding me of my promise. But after a pause, she yells, "Thanks!"

Five lake kids arrive in a cluster, laughing about something someone said or did, then a few guys trickle in between the torches. Most of the boys I recognize from school. A couple of younger siblings trail behind them. Like me, lake kids are usually responsible for their younger brothers and sisters at night and on weekends, when parents work in retail stores, restaurants, or the lumber mill forty miles east of town.

Connor loops his arms around two girls in the group. "Who wants to help me gather firewood?"

The girls don't giggle or bounce their hair. Lake kids aren't like the California girls Connor claims act a certain way. I have a difficult time believing Connor's version of California girls exists. Nobody is that eager to please.

Three guys jog down the trail tossing a boomerang that slices over the dock. My eyes stick to the blade, cutting air close to Grace's head.

Umé reads my mind. "Do they even see Grace on the dock?"

When the boomerang inches by her body, I jump to my feet and shout, "Watch where you're throwing that thing! You almost hit my sister!"

"Sorry, Aggi!" a guy named Troy shouts.

Another boy jogs beside me and mumbles, "Sorry about that, Ag."

A third guy pops over my shoulder, and I raise my hand before he has a chance to apologize. I'm used to soaking up sympathy but tired of it, too. Once, I was just Aggi, a cute-on-good-hair-days girl, but now I'm a tragedy, that dead girl's sister, that girl with the dad who smashed his best friend's face into a truck, the one with the strange mom who wanders the college campus talking to her daughter's ghost. I'm the grieving girl everyone feels like they should apologize to when they realize they're having too much fun. I hate being that girl.

97

Umé mumbles, "Uh-oh," and I jerk my neck toward the dock. "Nope. Wrong way." She motions toward the house with her thumb. "Look over there, or maybe you shouldn't."

I shift to the side of my chair as Max strolls down the path with one hand stuffed in his front pocket, the other bopping the top of each torch stand, quenching fires, then making the flame burn bigger and brighter, like a goddamn magician. He's layered from head to toe. Belted dark pants tapering just above his boots. A dark blue plaid flannel shirt peeking from the bottom of his sweater. His coat sleeves tied around his waist. A black knit hat. Fingerless gloves. Sideswept bangs. Oh my God. Max is here.

When he reaches the clearing at the lake, Henry shoots me a mixed look of *holy shit* and *this could be fun*. I shake my head at Henry and scowl. He shrugs as if to say sorry, then drops his head and smirks at his feet.

Umé leans forward, elbows on knees, and whispers, "Should we go?"

I yank the hat from my head, and my hair spills onto my shoulders. "No way," I say loud enough for Max to hear. "We were here first. He's the one who should go."

13

GO? I JUST GOT HERE.

And where would I go, anyway? Back home to circle the driveway like I was doing when Henry texted me? His message, urgent: *She Who Must Not Be Named is at Connor's. Where the hell are YOU?*

It took me over an hour to finally text Henry back that I was on my way—right after I finished circling my driveway, making a decision that could potentially kill me or change my life.

When I finally committed to return to Connor's, another twenty minutes was necessary for me to get ready. I raced inside the house and slipped into a button-up and the sweater Aggi bought me for my birthday—the one she said I looked sexy in—then shot my clothes with cologne. Pawtrick Swayze sneezed, confirmation that a second spray was not needed. I mean, I am not Connor.

I expected Aggi to be at Connor's when I arrived, just not sitting in that wooden chair looking like she'd been brushed by an artist. Her soft lines blending into the backdrop of the lake. Light from the torches meeting the moon's glisten. Aggi, right there in front of me and I'm not hiding. I'm standing and staring and out in the open. I'm also breaking a restraining order, adding red ink to legal paperwork, but I'm frozen. In fear. In love. A mixture of both.

The sky's almost black except for the dot-to-dot of stars popping in and out of passing clouds. I wish I played the guitar like Cal did at lake-kid parties. When I was young, he was always strumming on the porch in the evenings, Aggi and I calling out songs by obscure bands, never able to trip him up. He knew every song ever made. Old-school Elvis. Eighties R.E.M. Nineties grunge. And a lot of Twenty One Pilots. I wish I had asked Cal to teach me how to play something swoon-worthy, if for no other reason than to busy my fingers when I showed up to a party empty-handed. I could be sitting in that chair beside Aggi, plucking strings, but I'll probably never be that close to her again.

"Hey, Max!" Troy yells, and I wave.

Another guy from school jogs up and holds out his hand. We pound fists, and he begins to make small talk. I have no idea what he's saying. My focus is Aggi. Her sudden arm movements, mannerisms, ease. She's talking to Umé, and I wonder if she's uncomfortable that I'm here. The last thing I want to do is make her uncomfortable.

I consider walking back to the house, but Aggi stands and my eyes are drawn to her face. Her arms motion toward the dock. Is that Grace? She's too close to the water to not be wearing a life vest. I glance around the crowd, back at Aggi. Is anyone even watching that little girl?

"Maxwell, hi, hello." Umé's voice causes me to jump. I straighten my spine and glance over again at Aggi. Her head shifting back and forth between Umé and the dock.

"Umé, my friend. What's up?"

"Hello, Maxwell. Need you to be quiet and listen."

I nod.

"Henry set this up. Didn't he?"

I shake my head. "Don't know what you're talking about."

Umé steps forward, and I step back.

"What do you propose we do now?"

My head shakes. "Are you and Aggi going to leave?"

"Why would we leave?" Umé drags the heel of her boot across the ground.

"Just so you know, I technically was here first but had to run home for reasons I can't divulge."

Umé rolls her eyes. "We heard all about what you forgot at home. Your balls. Am I right?"

I fake laugh, extra deep.

"Look. You know the routine. Aggi's not ready to talk."

My stomach flips. "You mean she wants to? Just not yet?"

101

Umé parks her hands on her hips and twists around toward Aggi. "I can't answer that. Not right now."

"So there's an answer?"

Umé turns to walk away, and I reach for her shoulder.

She whips around and sighs. "I'm as sure of what to do as you are, but just don't do something you'll regret, okay? Maybe stop following her around."

"But we're on private property and we've both been invited here. There's no law preventing us from being here together!" My voice crescendoes in the quiet woods and grabs Henry's attention as he's warming his hands over the fire pit.

"All good, Maxwell?" he shouts.

I swat Henry's question away and picture myself stepping up to a podium, tapping the microphone, and hushing the crowd. Umé's right. I need to stop following Aggi. I shouldn't have to keep my distance. I should be able to walk beside her, not pretend to jog laps at the college or dive behind trees. Now is the time to stop hiding how I feel. And if Aggi turns away, shouts that she sees me as her father does—blameworthy like my dad—I will leave her alone. But I must hear it from her.

14

Aggi

MAX LOOKS UNBELIEVABLY HOT TONIGHT. Extra hot, hot-sauce hot. But he's pacing, pointing his finger in the air, and slinging words like "private property," "law," and "us being here." I scoot to the edge of the wooden chair. I should go. Clearly he's angry we're here, but if I shout Umé's name, Max will look in my direction.

I slide out of the chair and around the back side for a clearer yet more casual view of Umé and Max. Henry's standing, too, rubbing the back of his neck and turning in circles beside the fire pit. He's unsure what to do. He glances my way and waves. Henry must have have known about the possibility of Max and me showing up at the same party, and I can't help but wonder how much of this was planned.

Max lifts his finger like he's declaring war, peace, independence. He glances in my direction, and I stare at the back of a chair. He turns toward Umé, and I step toward them, realizing nothing prevents me from walking up to my friend and asking if she wants to stroll out on the dock. I could move closer to Max. My dad is at home. It's not as though he's lurking in the trees ready to pounce as I move toward Max. Nobody holds me in place. Nothing is stopping me.

At the hospital, in the moments after Cal died, Max and I were connected. Our hands webbed and our arms intertwined. I remember my tight grip around Max's fingers, as if my hand knew loosening would mean letting go of him forever. Paperwork that ordered us to keep our distance had not surfaced. Lawsuits did not exist. There were no lines Max and I couldn't cross.

For those short and tender minutes, my parents wanted to be with Max's family. My mother held Max's mother, and she melted against my mom's chest. My dad and Mr. Granger shook as they cried in each other's arms. Love held us together as one large family. No one spoke, not even Max and me. He sat, staring at the wall, and I stared along with him.

But after the doctor released Kate to go home, guilt moved in with us. It whispered at Kate's ear when she turned out her bedroom lights. Kate blamed herself for Cal's death. She suffered and could not let go of the guilt she felt for losing control of the vehicle as it spun on ice. Dad told Kate it was not her fault. Mom said blame belonged to nobody. But Kate stared at my parents, her big glassy eyes searching for an answer that would pull her out of the muddy waters swimming with guilt.

Convinced my parents could not see Kate's struggle, I dived headfirst into the swamp.

Kate sat on the strip of hardwood between her bed and her fuzzy blue rug, tucked in a tight ball, her head between her legs. She made a hiccup sound.

I dropped to my knees and rubbed her back. When we were little, Kate would draw on my back with her fingertip and I'd try to guess the letter. As I sat beside her, trying to explain what happens to moisture in the air before it tumbles to the ground and turns to ice, I spelled *I love you* over and over and over . . .

I used scientific terms, hoping to convince Kate that the weather was to blame, not her. I tried to sound like an expert. *Black ice is colorless. Transparent. Invisible. Loss of traction is sudden, especially on mountain bridges.* She tilted her head, and her eyes blinked. For a second, I believed I'd gotten through the guilt that held her down. But guilt is relentless, and I was weak and unprepared for the fight.

"I'll go where I want to go." Max.

"You're already doing that." Umé.

"What's that supposed to mean?" Max again.

"You follow her to work? You sit on your porch and stare at her house? If you care so much about her, why are you seeing other girls?"

I gasp and whip around toward Umé and Max. My sudden movement draws Max's eyes, flickering beside the growing bonfire. I step toward him.

Max stares at me while he answers. "I'm not seeing anyone."

"Not according to—"

"Hey!" a guy shouts from across the lakeshore. "Somebody help that kid!"

I jump toward the empty dock.

"Grace?" I shout as Umé races toward me.

"Where's Grace? Oh my God! Where's Grace?"

"Grace!" I scream, and sprint for the dock.

Footsteps pound behind me as I cut across the path, jumping logs and clumps of Kentucky bluegrass. Someone shouts, "Connor, get your flashlight!"

I'm a terrible sister. I should have been on the dock with Grace. She was there a minute ago. How many minutes ago? I can't remember the last time I checked.

Someone rushes in front of me with a torch in hand, yelling, "Grace! Gracie! Where are you, baby girl?"

Max.

I charge after him, shouting, "She was here a minute ago. Grace!"

The dock fills with people from the party swinging torches over the water. Max, flat on his belly, shines the torch onto the lake, and slides across the wood. Seconds feel like minutes, until someone shouts, "Right there!" and Max drops his torch into the lake, tears his boots from his feet, and dives into the black water.

"Grace!" I drop to my knees as Max springs from the lake,

water spraying from his nose and mouth.

Connor and two other guys race from the lakeshore and toss a tube at Max. "Here!" Connor shouts, but Max doesn't hear him. He disappears beneath the water.

I step to the edge of the dock and scream, "Shut up!" Voices hush, bubbles surface, as I scan the surface of the water. "Right there!" I point to the other side of the dock. Max's head bobs above the surface. "Grace!" His voice is tight from the cold water. He lunges for the tube, tucking it beneath his armpit.

"Over here!" I stumble over one of Max's boots and kick it into the water. "She's right there, Max! She's right there!"

"Shine the torches!" he yells, but his voice sounds weak.

"Shine the fucking torches!" I repeat, then yank a torch from Umé's hand and hover it over the water where Grace's coat surfaces.

Max goes under, his feet splashing cold water onto my legs. A couple of seconds and he's back at the surface. "She's here! I have her!"

I plug my nose and leap feetfirst toward Max.

15

SOMETHING CUTS ACROSS MY ARMS and breaks my grip from Grace's body. She's floating, facedown, her hair swimming like tentacles about her head. I flail, suck lake water into my lungs, and choke as Aggi scrambles toward her sister, gasping from the cold.

Aggi struggles, her body shocked by the cold water. I dive under and yank Grace by the waist as Aggi pulls her legs. We're battling against each other, but my mouth shivers too hard to offer direction, so I scoop Grace's head above water and she coughs as she draws a deep breath.

Aggi flaps her arm but doesn't go anywhere. I pull her away from Grace's body, fold Grace over my back, and push toward the dock. Aggi kicks my thigh as she reaches for Grace.

Henry and Troy swim up beside us with tubes. Henry scoops Grace up and swims for the dock.

When he reaches the wood, he moves Grace onto the dock with help from everyone's reaching arms.

"Where is she? Where's my sister?"Aggi twirls in the lake, slapping her tube and pushing it toward me.

"Hop on," I say, moving the tube in front of Aggi. "She's on the dock. She's fine."

I reach for the tube, holding it steady while Aggi drapes her arms across it and kicks her feet. Steering is impossible.

When we float against the dock, Henry and Troy reach for Aggi, but as she climbs onto her knees, she slips and falls through the tube's doughnut hole. I duck under the water and grab Aggi's waist.

"Let go of me!" she shouts, but I'm scared she'll slip away again, sink into the blackness of the lake.

"Let her go, Max," Troy says. "We got her."

Henry and Troy extend their arms toward Aggi's bobbing body.

Aggi swats at Henry's arm and grabs hold of the dock. She tries to pull herself up, but the cold-water cramps set in, and as she reaches for Henry, her wet hand slips from his grip. Henry falls on his ass.

"Give her a little push." Troy grabs Aggi's hand.

Aggi looks over; her teeth chatter, and her head nods. I scramble into action as though today I learned how to swim. First I fumble at Aggi's waist, unsure where to put my hands.

They splash around like a child until I reclaim my balls, though it's forty degrees and I'm in the middle of a lake. My muscles ache and I'm losing sensation in my legs, so I cup her ass with both hands and push with every working muscle fiber, and practically shoot Aggi over the dock.

16

MAX SMASHES MY BOOBS INTO the dock.

"Ouch!"

"Shit! I'm so sorry!"

Troy and Henry grab my wrists and drag me across the wood.

Umé wraps me in towels, but I scramble to my feet and crawl toward Grace's blanket-wrapped body.

"Are you okay?" I push Grace's wet hair to one side. Her lips tremble, teeth chatter.

"You two nearly ripped me in half," she snaps.

I glance back at Max, who's groaning as Henry, Troy, and another guy pull him from the water.

"You okay?" Troy and Henry ask in unison.

Max coughs, rubs his face with both hands, and fluffs his

hair. "I'm fine. Just make sure they are."

I clutch Grace in my arms, holding her close, as Max wrings water out of his sweater. The sweater I bought for him.

Troy hands Max a boot. "Sorry, man. Only found the one."

I gulp, remembering the boot I kicked into lake by accident.

Lifting Grace to her feet and squeezing her shoulder into my armpit, I snatch a blanket from Umé's hands and toss it to Max. It whacks him in the face and drops to his feet.

Max bends down, picks it up, and cloaks it over his shoulders like a cape. A tight smile squeezes, and I'm not sure if I smile back. Instead, I glance at the sky and the shooting star passing over Max's head. My mind blanks. A thousand wishes bombard my brain, but none coherent. There's only chaos.

Grace in the water. Mom's and Dad's tears. Screaming. Shouting. The thump of Kate's body hitting the floor. Max diving into water. The click of Cal's life support. Doctors and nurses and funeral directors. Then everything goes black. Complete darkness.

Max stares at me, and I refuse to look away. Five thousand reasons why I should dive into Max, grab him in my arms, kiss him, thank him for finding Grace. Five thousand and one reasons why I shouldn't.

Do it. Don't do it.

Kiss him. Ignore him.

Say something. Don't speak.

Dad and his blame. Will I ever be free?

"Let's get these girls to the hot tub," Connor shouts. "They need to be warmed up."

I lean into Grace. "Let's get you home."

Grace shakes her head. "You promised we could go hot-tubbing." She turns toward Umé and takes her hand. I shrug at Umé, unsure what to do as Grace yanks at my friend's arm as though nothing happened.

I slowly pass Max heading for the trail, and at the end of the dock, I turn. Max's head tilts, his eyes wide and welcoming. Voices echo as everyone follows the trail back to the house.

"You should probably get warmed up, too," I say.

Max shivers, uncertain how to—or if he should—respond.

I turn away from Max as my dad's voice grumbles. *You should have been watching out for your sister. What the hell were you thinking? What the hell were you doing with that boy? He's a distraction. If you hadn't been with him the night of the wreck . . .*

I sprint down the trail, calling after Grace.

At the house, Umé hands me my bag with our swimsuits and towels. She escorts Grace and me into the pool house, where everyone's changing in front of each other. I cover Grace's eyes with the blanket, and Umé shouts at the crowd, "Since when did we join a commune?"

Umé pounds on the bathroom door, and we wait our turn.

"You okay, Gracie?" Umé asks, rubbing her shoulders.

Grace grunts.

"And you?" Umé asks.

I nod. "I'm okay."

"Did you talk to Max?"

I exhale. "Not sure what I did."

Umé squeezes my shoulder and slips into the bathroom.

I drop to my knees, grab Grace's skinny wrists. "What happened, Gracie? Did you slip and fall into the water?"

Grace's eyes glaze as she fixes on a framed black-and-white photo on a stand beside the bathroom door. A picture of Connor as a little boy, holding hands with his dad as they walk along a pebbled beach. Grace's eyes well with tears. I wrap her in my arms, and she slaps my chest and pushes me away. I squeeze harder, but Grace squirms, wriggling to break free.

"Leave me alone, Aggi!"

"I can't. I don't want to."

She grabs my forearms, digs her nails deep into the skin.

"Don't tell them," she whispers.

"What? Who?"

"Mom and Dad. Don't tell them what happened tonight. I don't want them to know."

I nod, then shake my head.

"I mean it!" Now Grace rakes her nails across my wrists. "Promise you won't say anything."

"Okay." I nod. "I promise. I won't."

Grace glares, refusing to blink, even as her eyes pool with tears that spill onto her cheeks and run down her chin.

It is in that moment, when Grace makes me swear on my life, that I'm unclear if my sister fell from the dock or jumped on purpose. In my heart, nothing about this night feels like an accident.

17

WHEN I ASKED CONNOR FOR cocoa, I didn't mean cognac. I meant a damn cup of hot chocolate. But thanks to the drink, my lungs are now two million degrees and I'm no longer worrying about my boot lost at sea.

Instead, I'm staring at the pool house, eager for Aggi to emerge in her bathing suit. She's taking forever, and this girl I've known since elementary school, Rebecca, keeps inching next to me on the hot tub bench.

The door swings open, and Connor dives at Aggi. She picks his hand from her shoulder like a dirty napkin and says, "Thanks, but we need to go."

As I stand to climb out of the hot tub, Rebecca drapes her arms over my back. Apparently, she drank the same hot chocolate I did. I tuck my head to the side, try to slip out of her arms, and shout, "Hey! Connor!" for no reason other than to get Aggi's attention.

Aggi glances over as Rebecca jumps on my back and hooks me in a choke hold. My feet slip out from under me, and my shoulder slams against the hot tub bench.

Floating facedown is my only recourse. Aggi saw me. Probably heard me gag when Rebecca choked me. And now all I want to do is float into oblivion.

A hand grabs a clump of my hair and lifts my head above water. Henry's eye level, standing outside the tub. "You okay, bud?"

My feet fall in front of me as Rebecca shouts my name from the other side of the water. "I'll be right back, Max! Getting more hot chocolate!"

I nod, because that's what I do. Show everyone I agree while disagreeing on the inside.

Aggi watches Rebecca climb from the hot tub, snatch a towel, and head for the kitchen. "Yeah. We're definitely going."

I fall backward into the hot tub, splashing everyone sitting along the edge in their street clothes. It doesn't matter. If someone wants to kick my ass, let them. I'm exhausted inside and out. On my back, I stare at the black oily sky speckled with light until Henry's hairy foot jabs me in the ribs.

"I have an idea."

"Just let me drown," I moan.

Henry laughs. "Not in this lifetime."

18

WHEN GRACE WAS FIVE YEARS old, Dad took us to see beavers building a dam on the east side of Plum Lake. We cut through a steep section of the woods so Grace could stand high above the trees and view the lake as the birds do. Grace was always complaining about being too short or too little and wanting to grow.

Dad had made the trek with each of his girls for years, and it had become a rite of passage. When our legs were long and strong enough to make the journey, we'd set out for the hour-long hike. Grace's preschooler stumps zigzagged and wandered out of sight as she chased a squirrel into the brush, but Dad would stop and whistle, and Grace would rush over the pine straw, reaching for one of our hands.

Dad always announced our arrival with magical words.

"Would you look at that?" or "See what they've done?"

Dad scooped Grace up in his basket arms and motioned for Kate and me to take the lead. We stood side by side, mouths gaping, as we stared at the forty-foot dam emerging from the water's edge. The dam changed shape every time we visited the beavers, and Dad enjoyed spewing fun facts about an animal most of the lake people loathed.

Kate and I were about as excited to see a big pile of sticks as Grace was. We were there for the beavers. But if we were patient, the reward was worth the wait.

As we climbed up the footpath that led to the trail, we heard the splash.

"There he is!" Dad shouted, grabbing Grace by the armpits and plopping her over his head and onto his shoulders.

"Where, Daddy?"

"Where, Dad?"

"Where?"

Our eyes darted around the dam until Dad whispered, "There."

A slap of water rustled the grass near the edge of the lake, and we watched as swirling lines of water led us to a brownish-red doglike animal.

"He's still working," Dad whispered. "Means he hasn't found his mate yet."

"Mate?" Grace asked. "What's that?"

"A friend." Dad smiled and winked at Kate. "Like Aggi and Max or Kate and Cal."

Kate scoffed. "Uh . . . yeah . . . something like that."

We watched as the beaver gnawed bark from a fallen tree, scooped up straw and moss with his nose, and dumped it onto his back for transport.

Grace was mesmerized. The beavers made more of an impact on her than they ever had on Kate and me.

"How do you know it's a boy, Daddy?" she asked as Kate and I snickered.

Dad was patient, though, and answered every question Grace threw at him.

"Well, the boy beavers usually build the houses."

Kate groaned and Dad smiled.

"Sorry, Kate. Beavers adhere to sexist gender roles."

"When will he get a girlfriend?" Grace asked.

"Or boyfriend," Kate snapped.

"Well, I don't know," Dad said. "Maybe when he finishes the dam."

The beaver dived into the water, and Grace grew impatient.

"Where'd he go, Daddy? I don't see him."

Dad shuffled along the slope as Grace bounced on his shoulders, and he moved closer to the water's edge.

"Stay behind me, girls. We don't want to scare him away."

"Or get attacked by a beaver," Kate said, and Grace gasped.

"Yeah, his teeth are seriously long and sharp," I said, and Dad shushed me.

"Let's not scare your sister, girls."

"I don't see him, Daddy."

"Keep looking. Beavers can hold their breath underwater for fifteen minutes, maybe longer, before coming up for air."

Grace's eyes widened. "That's a long time, right, Daddy?"

"It sure is."

"Daddy?"

"Yeah, Gracie?"

"I'm going to be a beaver when I grow up."

19

Aggi

GRACE INSISTS WE DROP HER off at Dr. Nelson's, and on the way to the house makes me swear again I won't tell Mom and Dad what happened at the dock tonight. We lock pinkies and swear to the *beaver gods*—Grace's words.

When we arrive at Dr. Nelson's, she shoves pineapple upside-down cake at us, which we devour and chase with milk.

"This is the best damn pineapple upside-down cake I've ever eaten," Umé says, sucking her fingertips.

"It's the cherries," Dr. Nelson says. "Nobody uses the cheap maraschino cherries anymore. All this fear over red dye—"

"Red Number Four," Grace says flatly, her saucer lined with the cherries she picked from her cake.

"I ate maraschino cherries when I was a kid. Drank the

syrup straight from the jar. And look at me." Dr. Nelson pats her stomach. "Healthy as a bloody horse."

"Dr. Nelson?" Grace says. "The average life span of a horse is thirty years."

Dr. Nelson and Grace lock eyes. Dr. Nelson has been a stand-in mother to Grace since Kate's death. They have a mutual respect, and when they stare at each other, one could get lost in the perplexity of love they share. The hard lines in Dr. Nelson's face soften, and her tightly drawn lips drop into a curve. "You're right, Gracie. Those cherries are probably bad for us."

I ask Dr. Nelson if I can borrow her hair dryer, and she nods without question.

"Second drawer to the right of the sink!" she shouts as I'm halfway to the bathroom.

"You're the best, Dr. N!"

"Tell me something I'm unaware of."

After tossing my clothes into the dryer and sipping two cups of hot tea with honey, I'm ready to continue the night with Umé.

Back in the kitchen, Grace holds a pinky in the air, and I assure her the secret is safe. It's not like what happened this afternoon would change Mom and Dad into concerned parents who listen to their kids and hug them in times of crisis. That's who they were before the crash. BC.

Bereavement-support pamphlets the hospital offered us said there was no perfect order to the grieving process. We

123

might experience anger, guilt, sadness, and shock. We could have crying spells (we did), headaches (yes), and trouble sleeping (still do). During the first few weeks after Kate died, any reaction was possible and normal. Dad's growing anger and Mom's distancing from Grace were normal reactions to the pain we all felt. Length of time, however, was subjective. One pamphlet said in six weeks we might start to feel better in some small way, while another pamphlet said there was no definitive timeline. I clung to those six weeks, though. Crossed days off a calendar in my room, and the closer we got to the six-week mark, the smaller the lump in my throat became. But nothing changed except that Dad got louder and Mom more withdrawn.

If I mentioned to my parents what happened with Grace tonight, fingers would be pointed. So my lips are sealed.

Grace nods, and I attempt to hold her gaze, but she turns her head and races down the hall squealing, "Dr. Nelson! Do you know what time it is?"

Dr. Nelson's voice booms, and I jump as she shouts, "It's Yahtzee time!"

Glimpses of baby Grace splash before me, and they all involve Max and our life on the lake.

Grace, no more than two years old, tumbling in the tall grass as she chased Max's new puppy, Pawtrick Swayze. A birthday present for Max. Kate and Cal were sitting on the porch together. Cal, strumming his guitar, hitting and some-times not hitting notes while Kate sang along. I wove around the yard as Grace chased me, laughing, tipping over, and as soon as she saw Max's new dog, she squealed and charged after it. "Puh-py. Puh-py."

My mother scooped Grace up in her arms, perched her on her hip, as Max's mom and dad joined mine in a quiet huddle that soon turned to laughter before splitting apart. My mom and Max's mom zipped up the front steps and disappeared into the house. My dad and Max's dad wandered off to the barn for a beer. Max's dad patted my dad's shoulder, their guts busting from belly-filled laughs. Me, Max, and Grace spent the day playing with the new puppy. It was one of the best days I can remember.

"I'm going to give the dog a tribute name," Max said.

"A tribute to what?" I asked.

Max's eyes lit up; his dimples popped. "Like a tribute band. But to you, Aggi. You and your favorite movie."

"Oh no! Please don't name him Baby."

Max burst out laughing and Cal jogged up behind us, swinging an arm around his brother's back. "What are you going to name him, Maxwell?"

"Aggi loves *Dirty Dancing*. It's her favorite movie of all time. Right, Ag?"

Cal tilted his head. "Of *all* time?"

I shrugged. I did really love that movie. Even as a young girl, and I still do.

"So I'm going to give my dog a tribute name. One Aggi will love."

Kate joined us, bending down and tickling the dog's belly as he plopped over onto his chubby side. We were standing in a circle with the dog in the middle.

"Well—?" Cal asked. "Don't leave us hanging. What are you going to call him?"

Max inhaled all dramatic-like and said, "Introducing my new basset hound, Pawtrick Swayze!"

"Pawtrick Swayze?" Cal and Kate laughed.

"What's wrong with it?"

Cal raised his eyebrows while Kate belly-laughed.

"Aggi?" Max asked. "You get it, right? The actor you like in that movie. Patrick Swayze."

I bent down on my knees, and Max's puppy climbed up my thighs and leaped at my face, his oversized tongue and ears flopping. "I *love* Pawtrick Swayze!"

Dr. Nelson shoves a plastic container of pineapple upside-down cake at Umé before we leave. She asks me three times to take some home for me and my family, but I refuse, insisting I'll stop by tomorrow if there are any leftovers.

"Did something happen at home?" Dr. Nelson whispers to me at the door. "Grace didn't want to stay at home tonight?"

I slowly nod and lock eyes with Dr. Nelson.

"Thought so," she says. "Well, come back if you need to. Don't care how late it is."

Dr. Nelson keeps a watchful eye on us as we climb inside the car. As we pull out of the driveway, Umé asks if we're going back to Connor's.

I remember how good Max looked walking along the trail from Connor's house to the lake, bopping the tops of the torches. How he leaned against a pine tree's stump, leg bent, foot flat against the bark. The breeze blew, shifting a blanket of glow from the fire pit to light up Max's body as he shifted his feet and went from shadow to spotlight, *Thank you, fire.*

Max dove into the water without hesitation. He acted on instinct. Grace was family. She was his sister, too. He even sacrificed a boot to save her tonight. I feel terrible about his boot.

I should have thanked Max before leaving Connor's house. There was a moment on the dock when I thought Max was hesitating, waiting for me to say something, like what he did meant so much to me. It was the first time we'd been alone since before Cal's funeral. Now I regret not saying more.

It was obvious Max wasn't with Rebecca in the hot tub. He wasn't flaunting a new relationship in my face. That's not the Max I knew before the accident. The one I caught a glimpse of tonight on the dock. Even if he is dating someone new, what business is it of mine? A goddamn year has passed, and Max still watches out for me, for Grace, but he sends mixed messages, too. At the lake, he looked right at me when he told Umé he wasn't seeing anyone, yet those girls at his house . . .

"We'd better not go back to Connor's." Though I feel pulled in opposite directions, returning to the lake party is a terrible idea. No matter how badly I want to see Max, I can't risk what might happen if I do. "I'd rather show you something amazing instead."

127

Umé and I hardly speak as we drive from Dr. Nelson's house into the center of the small college town. The side of the highway is snow-packed, but bare pavement shortens our drive to under twenty minutes.

When we arrive on campus, Umé protests with a series of "hell no"s.

"I hate college," she says. "The thought of four more years after four years of high school makes we want to barf. Besides, we're from the lake. And townies don't mesh well with lake kids."

I disagree with Umé. Kate would have fit in just fine at college. It was her plan. She loved books and adored learning. Piano was her passion, though, which is why she and Cal got along so well. They were both musicians. Kate learned to play the piano from an actual instructor, though, and Cal taught himself the guitar, but they connected, especially during the holidays when Mom made Kate play horrible Christmas tunes. Cal would jazz up the music with his guitar and deep, throaty voice. Kate would roll her fingers up and down the scale. They harmonized.

I wonder if Kate and Cal would still have written songs together after she went away to school.

THE HARMONY OF US

Lyrics by Kate Frank and Cal Granger

Surround us
When you're around us
We don't fight it
We willingly ignite it

And now we write songs and think about it
How does our story unfold?
The words you'll hear told
Will they grapple with your soul?

Take me
Take all
Turn me inside out and make me whole
Let my heart change the beat
Your words breathe
Consume me

You surround me as I'm around you
Is it time to move the clock?
Will you want what I want?
Surround me as I'm around you

This is the harmony of us
This is the harmony of us

20

"SO WHY THE SCIENCE BUILDING when we could be in a hot tub full of half-naked people acquiring flesh-eating bacteria or something worse?"

I fumble with my ID card and swipe it twice until the door beeps and unlocks. "Don't make me answer that question." Though I don't have an answer for Umé. Going to the rooftop was a spontaneous decision. The last time I was up there, the best and worst happened to me.

Umé and I climb the stairwell until we reach the top floor. Umé claims she's out of breath as she lingers on the stairs, staring at her phone screen.

"Who are you texting?" I call from the landing.

She ignores my question and quickly slides the phone into her pocket.

"Hold on!" she calls, stomping up the stairs. "My lungs."

I'm feeling the impact of my time in the lake. The plunge did damage to my insides that could take days to repair. I wonder if Max's lungs are burning from the cold, too.

I hit the metal door with my hip and lead us onto the roof. Chairs stack on top of each other, and black plastic wraps garden boxes filled with last season's dirt.

"Just a second." I jog to the other side of a metal box used to warm the entire science building. "Probably should stay away from that!" I shout over my shoulder, pointing at the whirling metal fan.

"You'd better be bringing back a pizza!" Umé shouts.

"Keep your voice down," I whisper-yell back. "The last thing we need is to get caught on the roof having a pizza party."

"So you *are* getting pizza?"

I slide my phone from my pocket and order a BLT pizza from Lucio & Sons, which will arrive in thirty minutes or money back, guaranteed. I rattle off the address but follow with: "I should probably just meet you at the back door that faces the parking lot."

I drag two lounge chairs over to Umé as she gazes onto the courtyard and campus.

"I can see why you talk about this place so much," she whispers.

The sky is black, but not as black as the sky above the lake. It's fuzzy with the glow from the streetlights. A perfect night to sit on the roof of the science building with your best friend and make memories that will replace old ones filled with heartbreak. I scoot a metal crate and center it in between our two chairs like an end table.

"Voilà!" I pull the cover off the crate to show Umé that we will be having heat soon.

"What the hell's a portable fire pit doing up here?"

"The roof acts as a storage unit. Look at all this crap!"

A rusty barbecue, two wheelbarrows—one tipped on its side—stacked metal crates, folding chairs, and miles of black plastic.

"Well, unless you've taken up smoking, we have no way to light a fire."

"Maybe I can find some matches in Dr. Nelson's lab." I trot over to the door. "Be right back!"

As I pull the handle, the door snaps back. I tug again, and the same thing happens.

"What the—?"

"What the hell?" someone shouts.

"Shit!" I plaster my body against the wall and the door swings wide, the toe of my shoe preventing it from smashing my face.

"Aggi?" Dr. Nelson says. "What are you doing here?"

I'd love to ask Dr. Nelson the same thing, but Grace slips through the open door and sprints onto the roof.

"This place is so cool!" Grace twirls in circles, arms outstretched as she takes in the view of campus.

Dr. Nelson cranes her neck over my shoulder as Umé jogs beside me and drapes an arm over my shoulder. "We were just leaving. Need to get back to my brother's dorm. Some dick threw my hat up here. Aggi was nice enough to help me retrieve it."

Umé hasn't learned lying to Dr. Nelson gets you nowhere.

Dr. Nelson clicks her tongue. "You shouldn't be up here, Aggi." She glances at Umé. "And especially not with your friends."

Clutching my hands, I begin to apologize. "I'm so sorry. I needed someplace quiet. I didn't want to go home, and this is the only peaceful place I know."

"You live on a lake, Aggi."

"But I needed a change of scenery." I drop my chin to show Dr. Nelson I'm filled with remorse. "I'm sorry." She may be my mom's friend and practically family, but she's still my boss.

Dr. Nelson grunts, and I ask, "Did you follow us here? Thought it was Yahtzee night."

Dr. Nelson's mouth opens, snaps shut, opens again. "Grace was worried about you."

I glance over at Grace, spinning circles in the few patches of snow left unmelted on the roof. "Sure she was."

"You showed up at the house with wet clothes and hair. What else was I supposed to do? Ignore the signs of trouble?"

A car crunches snow in the parking lot below the science building, and Umé and I exchange glances. *Pizza delivery. Now we're screwed.* The car door slams and footsteps crunch. Dr. Nelson walks over to the railing. "Pizza?"

I cover my mouth as someone pounds the metal door below us.

We follow Dr. Nelson as she stomps down the first flight

of stairs. She hesitates at the landing. "Someone needs to stay out there and keep an eye on Grace."

I nod at Umé, and she saunters back up the stairs and onto the roof. Dr. Nelson flies from the landing, bounding two steps at a time in steel-toed boots. On the bottom floor, she kicks the door open like a badass professor.

"That'll be nineteen fifty," Lucio & Sons' pizza guy says, shoving the pizza box at Dr. Nelson.

"Wrong dorm, bud—this is the science building."

"Dr. Nelson?" I say, my voice squeaky. "So . . . uh . . . I ordered pizza. Sorry again. I really needed to be here tonight. To feel like a whole person and not the sliver of pie nobody wants. I needed to eat pizza and stare at the sky and talk about things that make me happy."

Dr. Nelson's hand slips off her hip. Her face softens.

"You of all people," I continue, "actually, probably only you, would understand."

Everything I say is truth. I can't lie to the only adult in my life who's given a damn about me and Grace since Kate died.

Dr. Nelson exhales. "What'd you say the price was again?"

Lucio & Sons' pizza guy stares at the receipt, then at Dr. Nelson. "Nineteen fifty, ma'am."

Dr. Nelson yanks out the wallet chained to her back pocket. She slaps thirty into his hand. "Keep the change."

"I have money," I say, and she holds up a finger to shush me.

"I'm paying, but I fully expect you to share."

21

MAX

"THIS IS A TERRIBLE IDEA," I tighten the laces on a pair of tennis shoes Henry grabbed from the bed of his rusty Chevy pickup. They are two sizes too big and wet inside, and my big toe keeps popping out of a nickel-sized hole, but I am in the parking lot of the science building with the truck engine running, desperately trying to keep my shit together.

"Umé thought you and Aggi could talk," Henry says. "In a private place without the risk of someone who knows Aggi's dad seeing you."

I rub my temples. "But what did Aggi say? She didn't act like she wanted to talk at Connor's."

"Well, Rebecca *was* draped over your back."

I groan.

Henry shrugs. "You jumped into the lake to save her sister!

135

Believe me, Aggi wants to talk."

"But you know this how?"

"I just do."

I drop my head against the window. "Sure hope you're right, because if you're not . . ."

Henry's right about a lot of things. When your home life and the people you live with are as chaotic and unpredictable as Henry's—twin brothers who resolve disagreements with backyard mixed martial arts—you become an expert on seeking out refuge and places of comfort. The four of us—Henry and Umé, me and Aggi—found comfort in each other. Our friendship was smashed to pieces when my dad's lawyer said it would be best if all family members kept their distance. When Aggi and I ended, the relationships we all had—Henry and Aggi, Henry and Umé, me and Umé—ended, too.

"Will you tell me the truth?" I ask, and look over at Henry.

"Always."

I knuckle my forehead, focus on my words. "One minute you suggest I move on, try new things, which I assume means see other people, and I tried, Henry, but nothing about it feels right. Then the next minute, you imply I could have a future with Aggi and I shouldn't give up." I half smile, wondering if I'm concealing the irritation stirring inside me. Not at Henry, but at the situation, and the frustration I feel.

Henry sighs. "Sometimes I see how confused you are and I think, wouldn't it be better if you and Aggi were through?"

I chuckle nervously.

"But then I see the way you defend Aggi when Connor says something disgusting about her. I see the spark in your eye, Max, when someone says her name. How you look at her, searching for an opening that will bring you back together. We can't fix the past, but we can always fight for a better future and what makes us happy. Shit, you know I'll always war for love."

Henry slumps against the door, staring out the window and chewing his bottom lip. At home, Henry witnesses a lot of fighting, yet he remains hopeful. My parents love each other. They love me. Yet I'm filled with frustration, as I think they should act differently. Henry's father has been arrested three times this year for busting up property and people. His oldest brother sits in the county jail for breaking the bridge of someone's nose, and Henry's twin brothers are constantly beating him up for no reason. That's how Henry's family resolves their issues. Henry's father sends the kids outside to fight and tells them not to return until shit's handled. Henry never throws a punch. He says, "They're my brothers. I can't bring myself to hurt them." Henry is much bigger than the twins. He could take down either one. Some might say Henry has the right to protect himself—I've said it—but they are not Heart-of-Gold Henry.

"You remember when my dad forbade me to hang out with you after your brother died?"

Henry is the only person who admits that my brother died. People—even me—mention the "accident" or the "tragedy," but Henry confronts the truth. I nod and stare at the dash.

"Fear," Henry snaps. "Selfishness, too, or maybe self-centeredness. I don't know which, but I guess it doesn't matter. My dad didn't want me around you. You know why?"

I nod. "Fear. Selfishness."

Henry chuckles. "You'd spoken to the police. The cops popped up on your property unannounced. When you have things to hide—stolen things—you don't want your kid hanging with people the police visit."

I laugh. "Like your dad or his stolen Porta-Potty were on my mind."

Henry rubs the bridge of his nose and winces. "Yeah, that's what I told him, but my brothers insisted I was going to rat them out."

"Which one did that?" I tap my nose.

Henry clears his throat. "Doesn't matter. They're both scared of me. They know it takes two of them to take me down."

I tilt my head, letting Henry know I'm eager to listen if—and when—he wants to talk. Henry's always been there for me. This past year, he hasn't left my side, even in the wake of his father's warnings.

"That's why they do it," Henry continues. "Mama's not around to referee anymore,"

I drop my head, remembering sixth grade, when Henry lost his mother to cancer.

"Your mama made the best fudge."

Henry glances over. "You remember that?"

"Shit yeah. How could I forget? Remember when we ate the whole platter she'd made for my parents? Remember how big that platter was? How sick we were?"

"I shit for days." Henry laughs.

"Oh God, me too."

"What I'd give for another bite."

We both nod, neither saying a word.

I don't know much about Henry's mother except that she always called him Henry, not Hank. She got pregnant very young, then married Van Bobby Beacon, Walabash Woods's finest specimen. (Cough, cough) Henry says people warned his mother that Van Bobby Beacon was bad news, but she thought she could change him.

Henry's mother, Cynthia Kristine Riggs, left his father a few months before Henry was born. The twins must have been three years old, Henry's oldest brother eight, when a very pregnant Cynthia Riggs boarded a plane headed for Honolulu. Henry doesn't divulge why his mother left, although I can imagine a few hundred reasons. She showed up at her parents' home in Hawaii with sad eyes and begged them to bury the hatchet. Henry's grandparents—both professors before they retired from where Dr. Nelson teaches—had cut ties with their daughter when she married Henry's father.

Henry swears he's going back to Honolulu one day. If his mother could peddle enough fudge at farmers markets and businesses in town to buy a plane ticket out of Walabash

Woods, Henry insists, he'll do the same.

"It's where my heart is," Henry always says. "Where I belong."

Henry spent six months in Hawaii (half that time living in a womb) before Van Bobby Beacon begged his wife to return to Walabash Woods, using false hope and fucked-up promises. But when Henry shares the story, it sounds as though he's lived in Hawaii his entire life. When Henry meets a new girl from town and they ask where he's from, guess what he says? "Where the wind tastes like coconuts."

"Well," I say breaking the silence, "thanks for the shoes, bud."

Henry nods. "Poor Grace. And Aggi. Did you see the worry on Aggi's face?"

Pure terror. I can't think about what would have happened had I not been there. Not like I'm some kind of hero. I just reacted the way anyone else would have.

"Everyone's been through so much," Henry says with a sigh.

"Yeah, and I feel like I should say thanks a million times." Henry raises his eyebrows. "You're always there for me. For Aggi. I just . . . I'm just . . . really glad we're friends."

Henry grins. "Likewise."

"You know," I say, drawing a deep breath, "there's something I want to talk to you about, but I'm fucking embarrassed."

Henry sits up and offers me his serious face. The long

140

pause encourages me to continue.

I exhale, clear my throat. "You know Aggi and I . . . you know that night . . . of the accident?"

Henry furrows his brow. "I guess?"

"Well, ever since Cal . . . and then Kate died . . ." I stop. Unsure how to proceed or even if I should, but Henry nudges me with his head.

I draw another deep breath. "Well, that night of the accident . . ." I can't. I haven't shared these private details with anyone. Not even the therapist. I know Henry won't judge me or laugh or say anything that makes me more uncomfortable than I already am, but I'm afraid of the vulnerable feeling you get when you open yourself up. There is always some degree of uncertainty how the person will react.

"The night of the accident, you and Aggi were together. I know that," Henry says. "And you know it wasn't your fault. It wasn't Aggi's and it sure wasn't yours."

I nod. "Yeah, but since then . . . I mean, I'm a shell. I feel so empty."

Henry shifts sideways on his seat. "I'm no counselor, but you lost your brother, man. Emptiness is your normal. At least for now."

"Yeah." Hearing someone else say these words comforts me. Like maybe these hollow feelings won't last forever.

"I remember the school counselor talking to me after my mother died. She said when we lose someone we love, a hole forms in our heart. Mind you, she was talking to an

141

eleven-year-old, and I envisioned a literal hole in my chest where my heart once beat. But she said the hole was normal. That it wouldn't destroy me. It would only make me feel empty for a while. She didn't pretend to know how long I'd feel this way, and I'm glad she didn't lie or feed me a bunch of bullshit like *time heals all wounds*, though I suppose it does heal some. My point is that what you're going through—how you're feeling—isn't out of the ordinary. It's *your* ordinary."

I fidged and pat the seat. "Yeah. Some people go numb like my mom and dad. And others . . . well, let's just say, I've lost sensation in some places, too."

Henry looks confused.

"I am empty," I say. "Really fucking empty."

"I bet."

"And I'm numb. Sometimes I'm just like my parents when they stare at the television and laugh at things that aren't funny."

"I understand."

"And I haven't been able to get an erection since Cal died." My face heats. Immeasurable embarrassment. I cup my hands over my face and groan, which only adds to my humiliation.

Henry draws a breath but says nothing. I think I hear him swallow.

A car engine revs beside us, and I look up. Lucio & Sons pizza delivery.

"O-kay," Henry says. "All part of the process."

I stare at the floorboard. The old Max, the one springing

142

boners right and left, would have busted out laughing by now and shouted, *Joke! Just fucking kidding!* But the Max of today, the one on the verge of giving up on myself and my future, sits still and listens to the *ping-ping* of water droplets hit the windshield. I am drowning in humiliation.

Henry sniffs and wipes his nose. "Seriously. I think it's part of the loss, or the guilt you feel over losing someone you love."

I shake my head.

"I don't mean *that*." Henry motions at his crotch, and I wince. "Let me clarify. You have to look at the timeline. I'm not at all surprised. Are you?"

"I don't know," I mumble and hold my head.

"This is really messing with you?"

Silence.

"Well, you haven't exactly had another opportunity."

I groan, unsure how to explain that I've had many opportunities.

Henry switches to his doctor voice. "Have you tried other methods?"

I chuckle. "Yeah. I've tried all methods."

A ridiculously long pause ensues, followed by Henry's cheerleading voice.

"I hear it's like a bicycle. Once it's happened, it *will* happen again. You have to give it time. Some people get holes in their hearts. Others, well . . ."

We smile at the floorboard.

"I believe when the time's right, when your mind's clear,

and you're not under so much stress . . . I mean, you've got a lot of shit on your plate, Max . . . but give it some time. Life will *rise* again."

We side-eye each other, expressionless, then burst into laughter. I mean, what the hell else are we supposed to do?

Henry refuses to leave us feeling awkward for long. He grins, slaps the steering wheel with an open palm, and says, "Let's go find our friends."

22

Aggi

AFTER SLICES OF PIZZA, THE four of us are laughing and crying and expressing just how much we love science and one another. Well, Umé doesn't exactly say she loves science, but she's at least playing along without protest. Dr. Nelson retells stories from her high school years and has Grace and Umé sitting on the edges of their chairs begging for more.

"There was that time," Dr. Nelson says, "when we broke into the biology lab at our high school on a rescue mission we called Save Life. Worms and frogs and, I think, a few dung beetles found themselves rescued and given freedom in a pond near my family's home."

Dr. Nelson's face beams with pride from remembering yesteryear.

"Same trope, different decade, huh?" Umé says. "Kids

145

have been rescuing mice and frogs since forever."

Dr. Nelson winks. "It's an oldie, but we made it our own. Still puts a smile on my face." Dr. Nelson shoves the cardboard box at us. "Come on, kids, eat another slice so I don't slip into a carb coma alone."

I grab my stomach and groan. "This is my second dinner, and the first was huge."

"So how'd you become a biologist, then?" Umé asks. "If you couldn't handle keeping animals captive?"

Dr. Nelson flicks a crumb off her pants. "That was a long time ago."

"Did you get caught?" Grace asks. "Did your teachers find out about your rescue mission?"

"I got into a bit of trouble with the police. Thanks for asking." Dr. Nelson winks at Grace and taps her on the knee. "Took a gap year before college on account of it. Let's just say I've done my fair share of community service."

Umé pulls her knees to her chest. "You're a professor now. Couldn't have been that bad. Breaking and entering? Destroying school property?"

"Let's just say the rescue mission grew into something bigger as the night went on."

Our faces contort. "Bigger?"

Dr. Nelson sighs. "Long story. One I'd rather not get into."

Umé leans forward in her chair, elbows on her knees. "But one we have time for."

Dr. Nelson rubs her arms in an attempt to change the

146

subject. "So cold out here. We should head home before it starts snowing again."

Umé kicks at the metal fire pit. "Can't we light this thing?"

Dr. Nelson shrugs and reaches into her bag, pulling out a small orange box of matches with black lettering that reads: *Take a poop? Light a match.*

After a couple of strikes, the fire pit roars and we hover around the circle listening to Dr. Nelson divulge details we desperately want to hear. Well, except Grace. She's been sent to the other side of the roof to search for something that doesn't exist. Another one of Dr. Nelson's missions, titled Protecting Innocent Ears.

"We didn't plan to hurt the poor bastard," Dr. Nelson whispers. "We only wanted to save the beavers."

"Hurt who?" I ask, warming a narrow slice of pizza over the fire until the cheese melts.

"You know him, Aggi. Well, you know of him. Your friend Henry Beacon's grandfather." She pauses, glances over at Grace.

"She's okay. Keep going." Umé's always loved a good tale, and Dr. Nelson has many. We could be here all night.

"Well, we were pretty proud of ourselves—me and my three girlfriends—and when we finished dumping the critters off at their new home, we felt alive and powerful and like we wanted to do something more." Dr. Nelson takes a breath. "That's when we should have stopped."

147

"But you didn't?" Umé's eyes widen with anticipation.

"Nope. We kept it going." Dr. Nelson looks over her shoulder at Grace, now chopping snow with a stick.

"Don't leave us hanging, Dr. N," Umé says, untwisting her scarf.

The fire crackles and Dr. Nelson scoots her chair back to avoid the smoke blowing in her face. I glance over at Grace to make sure she's wearing gloves.

"There were these rumors around the lake," Dr. Nelson whispers. "The Beacons and their beaver traps. If they caught one, they pummeled it to death and sold off the pelts."

Umé gasps, and Dr. Nelson nods.

"I don't like where this story is going," Umé says. "I've no use for animal abusers. Right, Aggi? No damn use!"

Dr. Nelson nods again. "Exactly! So we decided to act on what we'd heard. We were all dressed in black—boots like the ones I'm wearing—and we were ready to smash those traps. Should have left things alone, but . . ." She tucks a strand of hair behind her ear, and it springs forward.

"Did you rescue a beaver?" Umé asks.

"It was hell getting close to the water where we'd heard the traps were set, but long story short, we found them. Then old man Beacon found us."

Umé covers her mouth and groans.

"When we saw the traps were empty, we smashed them to bits with hammers and shovels we'd taken from my family's toolshed. The noise must have echoed. We weren't exactly quiet. We were exhilarated. It felt like we were doing something that mattered."

Umé and I nod.

"Before long, we heard his shouts and took off running. We split apart, but one of us got caught." Dr. Nelson bites on her lip. "I'll give you one guess who that person was."

"You!" we both shout.

Dr. Nelson stands and takes a bow.

"What'd he do?" I ask. "Because if he's anything like his son or grandchildren . . . well, except for Henry."

"Oh, he was a meaner than hell. Teeth—the ones that hadn't rotted from his mouth—were as yellow as a beaver's, and when he grabbed me by my shoulders and shook, his breath stole mine away."

"Oh my God." Umé stands. "Please tell me you ran."

"I fought. Kicked and punched. I was afraid, but I wasn't about to die in the woods. When I finally broke free, he was shouting for me to run or he'd kill me. . . ."

Dr. Nelson stops, digs her fingers into her hair, and shakes her head.

"I got away. We all did. But two days later, the police found him. Dead. He'd died chasing me off his property."

"I heard about this!" I say. "Henry said his grandfather had a heart attack and died. He wasn't very old."

Dr. Nelson checks on Grace again. I follow her eyes and see Grace whacking a snowball across the roof like a hockey puck.

"I think he was just shy of fifty," Dr. Nelson says. "But old enough to know he shouldn't be trapping and killing beavers. There are humane ways to relocate the animals."

"Wow," Umé says. "When did the truth come out?"

Dr. Nelson sighs. "When I came clean and told my parents what had happened that night."

"But why?" Umé asks.

"Couldn't live with myself," Dr. Nelson says. "I had to confess."

"But he might have had a heart attack anyway," I say.

"We were there and we shouldn't have been. We could have reported the rumors we'd heard to the police. We could have done a lot of things differently, but we were just kids."

"From what Henry's said, his grandfather was pretty awful. He taught his son a thing or two about violence."

Dr. Nelson scoops a mound of snow in her hands and dumps it into the fire pit. "Not my best moment, girls."

Umé stands and scoops up a handful of snow. She shapes it into a ball and launches it softly at Grace's behind.

"Hey!" Grace shouts.

"Well, *we* think you're pretty badass, Dr. N," Umé says.

Dr. Nelson dumps more snow on the fire. "Not always but definitely now." She chuckles. "Sometimes you believe you're doing the right thing by bringing order to the chaos."

Dr. Nelson wanders over to the railing and slips an arm around Grace's waist. Grace wraps her arm over Dr. Nelson's shoulder and leans against her. They both stare up at the sky.

"Wait a second!" Umé shouts. "Did that shit go on your permanent record?"

Dr. Nelson turns around. "Permanent record?" She shakes her head and whispers, "We paid our debt. The only thing permanent is death."

Grace points across campus, but Dr. Nelson continues to whisper-talk.

"Like I said, not our best moment. But we felt relieved to get off as easy as we did. Community service for breaking into our high school. The judge was lenient on us with the Beacon incident. Sure, we'd been on private property, but those traps were illegal to begin with. Before long, we were all off to college and spreading our wings, but I still grapple with the guilt."

"Why'd you come back here to teach?" Umé asks. "You could be a professor anywhere."

A smile spreads across Dr. Nelson's face. "I could, and I have, but Plum Lake has a way of pulling you back—a gentle nudge, never with force—and when you're away from these woods and all the precious animals it contains, they're all you think about."

Umé reaches for Dr. Nelson's hand. "Will you adopt me?"

I pop up behind Umé. "Get in line."

We're all gazing across the campus and courtyard—bellies full of pizza—taking in the newfound beauty of our surroundings when Dr. Nelson belches and says, "Pardon," in her best French accent and we burst into laughter.

"Hey!" Grace shouts. "Those headlights have been shining our way for a very long time."

Dr. Nelson leans over the railing. "No one should be here. We shouldn't even be here. Who, besides me, studies science on a Saturday night?"

"Another professor?" Umé asks, removing her glasses and rubbing them on her scarf.

"That truck looks a lot like Henry's," I say.

Umé grabs my shoulder. "Seriously?" She grips the rail. "Holy shit! It is!" But her voice sounds forced and makes me think Umé expected them to be here.

"Aggi's stalker returns," Dr. Nelson says.

"Returns?" Umé says. "He never leaves."

Dr. Nelson drapes her arm over my shoulder and gives it a firm squeeze. With my best friend on one side, Dr. Nelson on the other, Grace bouncing between us, I'm wrapped in safety, security, and calm. It's the most whole I've felt in a year.

"You know that boy cares deeply," Dr. Nelson says at my ear. "Why else would he shadow you wherever you go? He thinks he's watching out for you, honey. Consider it a compliment."

I stare at Henry's truck. The headlights beaming.

"Dad says Max is trying to dig up information he can give to his father's attorney. He's forbidden me to ever speak to Max again. He said if I did, he'd hurt him."

Dr. Nelson scoffs. "Oh, is *that* what your dad says?"

I nod. "As much as I want to talk to Max, I can't. It would ruin dad's countersuit."

"Well, wouldn't that be a goddamned shame!"

Dr. Nelson slides her arm off my shoulder and squeezes my hand.

"With all due respect, Aggi, your dad doesn't know shit."

23

MAX

AFTER OUR FIFTH MARCH AROUND the science building to check each door for access, Henry says, "I think I forgot to turn off the headlights."

A student jogs toward us on the sidewalk. My teeth chatter, and I'm struggling to keep Henry's shoes on my feet every time I shuffle-step. "Just leave them on. We won't be long." I'm not about to return to the truck now and let this student slip past me.

"Hey!" I shout. "Can we borrow your ID card?"

The jogger yanks off his hood and trots backward. "Sorry, but that's a hard no." He turns and disappears into the campus.

The sky begins to spit light flakes of snow, and the vacant grounds in front of the science building remind me it's late. As we approach the main doors, a voice sounds from the roof.

Henry yanks the handles for the hundredth time. "I'm texting Umé. She said she'd watch for us and let us in."

"Let's wait here." I blow on my hands, taking a step back for a better view of the roof, and trip on Henry's sled-shoes.

Henry's typing on his phone as I slide my feet across the sidewalk, craning my neck. Someone's laughing above us. My heart revs as I think of the last place Aggi and I spent time alone together.

"Come on!" Henry shouts, banging on the door. "Open up!"

I'm skiing my way back to Henry when a light flashes and a loud throat clears. "Door's locked, Einstein."

I whip around and come face-to-face with a black-haired, red-lipped, green-eyed girl with arches in her eyebrows that put ski jumps to shame. "ID card?" she snaps, and her blue-painted nails poking from her fingerless glove shimmer beneath her flashlight. Henry joins me on the sidewalk.

"ID card?" Henry and I repeat like a couple of high school kids in the presence of a college girl.

The girl rolls her eyes and, with an extraordinary amount of effort, slides her left hand out of her back pocket and reaches inside her coat. She retrieves an ID card and fans it in our faces. "Looks something like this."

"Oh, yeah," Henry says. His voice shaky and frog-like. He clears his throat. "We left ours . . . our ID cards . . . at our dorm. But it's great you brought yours. Can we use it?"

College girl stares at Henry. Henry starts to fidget. Sniffing, wiping his nose, making farting noises with his mouth.

The corner of the girl's mouth twitches. Is she smiling? At Henry?

"If you think I'm letting you in this building, you're mistaken." She shoves a second ID into Henry's face. "Campus security," she says.

Henry's eyes widen, his mouth agape. I know this look. It's the same one he gave when he first met Umé. Some might mistake Henry's droopy jaw, wide mouth, and big eyes for childlike innocence, but I know better. I know Henry. How he's smitten by a strong girl with power, or in this case, an ID card that reads: *Jen Salazar—Campus Security*. She's dimple-cheeked and wearing black boots and a leather jacket, and as expected, Henry's about to lose his goddamn mind.

I glance at Jen, then back at Henry. She's slightly taller than he is. Her hand's back on her hip, and Henry's flashing a boyish grin. If these shoes would stay on my feet, I'd kick his shin and snap him out of his insta-love stupor.

"I . . . I . . ."

I shuffle next to Henry. "What Henry means is that we . . . I . . . left my bag upstairs in the science building and my ID card is in it. That's the whole problem."

Jen looks at me like she's unimpressed. In fact, she yawns.

"And I suppose *his* card was in your bag, too?" Jen asks, and her eyes gravitate back to Henry.

"I . . . no . . . I . . . yeah . . ."

I sling a dagger with my eyes at Henry, but he keeps babbling.

"What my friend here is trying to say is that after an incredibly hard workout at the gym, we stuffed everything into one bag. His bag. My bag was left here by mistake." Henry's eyebrow lifts, and I squeeze his shoulder and continue my lie. "Then after our extremely difficult workout, we had bio lab, and I forgot my bag upstairs. Please have mercy on a fellow college student. My whole life, including my ID card, is in that bag."

"The bag that's upstairs?" Jen's brow furrows.

I nod. "Yep. Yeah. Yes, ma'am."

Jen hesitates, glances at Henry again, and sighs. "Okay. I'll probably regret this, but let's go get your bag." She swipes her card in the door, and the light shifts from red to green. She jerks the handle and holds the door open with her hip. "You coming or what?"

Henry and I freeze. What do we do now? How do we find a fictitious bag?

But with Aggi on the roof, I'm pulled indoors. If we get busted, at least I'll know I tried to talk to her.

We move into the doorway, and Henry whispers, "Holy hell. This girl is amazing. Come on, let's go."

"Go where exactly?"

"We'll figure it out when we get there," Henry whispers. "Act like you know what you're doing."

"Second or third floor?" Jen asks, marching toward the stairs.

"Isn't there an elevator?" I ask, but Jen doesn't hear me.

157

Henry bounces past me, and I grab the back of his coat. "I have no idea what we're doing. Do you?"

Henry grins. "Following Brienne of Tarth. Now come on!"

Henry races up the stairs, two at a time, while I struggle to keep the shoes on my feet with each step.

At the third floor, Jen opens a door and hesitates. When I finally reach the landing, she says, "Shoes are a little big, huh?"

I purse my lips and glare at Henry. Jen heads for the hallway, and Henry gives himself whiplash, signaling for me to get lost—down another hallway—so he can be alone with ~~Brienne of Tarth~~ Jen.

Henry fast-walks toward Jen, and I shoot down the opposite hallway, shouting, "I'll just go get my bag! The one I left somewhere around here!" As soon as I take off running, one of Henry's shoes slips from my foot.

The end of the hallway spills into a large room surrounded by glass and centered with potted plants and trees that spread their long, leafy branches toward the skylights. I shuffle to the left, then the right, scanning benches and chairs for a random backpack forgotten by a distracted student. I'm also taking my time to listen for voices. I half expect Aggi to jump out from behind a tree.

As I cross the corridor and enter a dimly lit hallway lined with faculty offices and locked laboratory doors, voices sound from behind a metal door that reads: *Rooftop Access*. A familiar laugh twists my stomach into knots and I practically

158

drop to my knees due to the sudden weakness throughout my body.

"Where'd he go?" *It's Jen.*

"Max likes to work alone. He's a loner. Quite the lonely guy." *Thanks, Henry.*

But it's true. So much of who I was disappeared after Cal died. My brother was the one I confided in, shared secrets with. He was the first person to know how I felt about Aggi. He even knew before Henry. And Henry knows everything about me.

Cal and I were brothers, but we were close friends, too. Sure, we had our sibling rivalry days when we were little, but Mom and Dad did a good job showing us we both mattered and didn't have to compete for attention. Cal was older, but never judgmental. He didn't act like the shitty older brothers you see in movies. He never looked down on me, thinking I was immature for not knowing what he did. Cal would just smile when I asked annoying-little-brother questions and strum his guitar. He made me feel like his equal. I loved when he'd put words into song and ask for my opinion.

Max, I wrote a new song. Tell me what you think.

Cal would have made an incredible dad one day.

One night, after I had come home from hanging out with Aggi, Cal sat on the edge of my bed, waiting while I brushed my teeth. When I walked into the room, he strummed his guitar and sang, *"Max loves a girl and she loves him."* Then he asked: "You do love her, right?"

I thought long and hard about the question Cal posed. He always asked the hard ones. The kind that made you examine life and the meaning of it. Questions that caused you to stop, turn direction, consider a whole new course.

I answered Cal with an adamant Yes! I loved Aggi. I was in love and wanted to stay that way forever. I didn't care that convention told me I was young and our love wouldn't last because we were "just kids." I refused to believe that. Love is completing and pain free when you're in the middle of its bubble.

But naysayers would pop in with: "You're so young. You have your whole life ahead of you. You should keep your options open."

I plugged my ears and thought, *What if my life ended, all of a sudden? What if I was driving to school, wrecked the Jeep, and died?* No more Max. At least I'd have fallen in love, known what it felt like.

Cal asked me if I was serious about Aggi, and I told him I'd never been more serious about anything in my life. He smiled and said, "Don't let that slip away." He could have told me I was young and had a lifetime of loves in front of me. He could have said, *Max, don't tie yourself down. You guys are both going to change through the years, and who you are now may not fit with who you'll become.*

Cal wasn't like that, though. He saw my heart on my sleeve and paid attention to how it beat in rhythm with Aggi's. When we ended our conversation, Cal asked if I thought Aggi felt the same way, and I said, "I think so." He strummed a beautiful melody and sang, "Then don't ever let her go."

Henry and Jen round the corner, interrupting my thoughts. Both laugh, their steps in sync. I plaster myself against the wall as Jen jabs at Henry's arm as if he's said something ridiculously funny, and I sigh at the tenderness of the scene. The two turn, and I dart to the dark side of the hallway. A small table shoved into the corner with a potted plant catches my eye, and when I step closer, I notice something sitting on top. A child's purse wedged between the wall and the stand.

As I approach the table, my foot slips out of Henry's shoe and lands with a thud.

"That you, Max?"

I snatch the bag, stuffing my arm through the tight hole and stake my claim by swinging it over one shoulder.

"Hey, guys!" I slide in front of Henry.

Jen eyeballs my purse. My purple kid bag outlined in sequins with the most gentle, squishable kitten I've ever seen. There's even fake fur.

"That's your bag?" Jen says mockingly.

"Yep." I pet the kitten. "One of my favorites."

Jen shrugs, and I shuffle toward the exit. Every damn step a challenge to keep Henry's shoes on my feet.

"Thanks for unlocking the door." Henry's voice is breathy, and the way he's looking at Jen with his droopy eyes and big smile makes me chuckle. Henry's always been a big believer in love at first sight, and since I'm a big believer in Henry, I support this. Henry used to explain to me how urgent love is, and I used to argue that love is a slow burn. It's one of the few things Henry and I don't see eye to eye on. But, of course, I'm biased. I fell in love with Aggi over the course of seventeen years. I measure love based on how it worked out for me, which, as it stands, blows a hole in my theory. But I'm holding on to hope. Henry believes connection can happen in a single conversation—a spark that kindles the heart—and out of that connection love is set in motion. When it comes to falling in love, Henry is urgent. Full speed ahead.

Jen smiles and says, "Gave me something to do until my shift ends in an hour. Then I'll be at my friend's party, remember? The one I mentioned upstairs to you."

Henry nods, chews his lip. "Well, have a great night."

I elbow Henry as Jen turns toward the door. He mouths, *Wow. She's amazing.*

I lean close to Henry and whisper, "She gets off in an hour. Friend's party. Clearly a hint. Ask her out."

"Out where?" Henry whispers. "She's a college girl. What the hell could I do with a college girl?"

I drop my jaw. "You really want me to answer that?"

Henry hisses, "For shit's sake, Max. I just met her."

"Exactly! Now ask her, or I'll do it for you."

"Ask me what?" Jen asks, holding open the door.

Henry's face lightens three shades. His freckles turn to embers. "Nothing."

Jen rocks the door back and forth, bumping it with her

162

knee. "O-kay. Well, I should go. You guys cool?" She pierces Henry with her dark eyes, and Henry squirms and shuffles his feet like a five-year-old in need of a bathroom.

After a long, painfully awkward pause, I say, "So where's the party?" and Henry gasps so loud Jen and I stare at him.

A slow smile appears on Jen's face as she says, "You're going to have to tell me your name first."

"Max," I say, then realize her eyes are on Henry.

"Hank. I mean, Henry. I mean, Hank?"

I pat Henry's back. "Friends know him as Henry. Those who aren't call him Hank."

Jen's eyes smile. "Okay, Henry?" And the way she says his name shoots Henry with a shot of courage I've had the privilege of seeing him unleash one other time in my life.

About six weeks after Kate's death, Henry and I were driving to my house. School had released early, and Henry had wanted to hang out. He stuck to me like glue during the weeks following my brother's death, and having him beside me softened the blow of Cal not being there. We were on the narrow road rounding the lake when Aggi's dad appeared out of nowhere. He drove up fast on our tail, flashing his high beams. Through the rearview mirror his hand waved for me to pull over. I parked the Jeep in the first plowed driveway I could find as Mr. Frank bolted from his truck. He was at my window shouting, "Get out!" before I had time to turn on the hazard lights.

Henry grabbed my elbow. "Lock your door. Don't get out!"

Mr. Frank had been like family to me, and I was used to doing what he said. There was no reason to distrust him. But he'd never raised his voice at me before.

I stepped onto the road, and like an avalanche, Aggi's dad spun me around and pinned me against the Jeep. My arm tucked behind my back, chest smashed against the cold metal, he kicked my legs out from under me, and I slid to the ground. At face level, he spit when he hissed, "You will stay away from Aggi! If I catch you with her again—"

"Let him go!" Henry shouted, jumping from the Jeep.

"This is no business of yours, son!"

Henry, overcome with adrenaline, charged Mr. Frank with fists raised. Henry didn't fly out of the Jeep intending to hit Mr. Frank; he saw an underdog and fought back. Henry lunged, and Aggi's dad released his tight grip on my wrists. My arm flooded with heat, and when I rolled to my side to get up, it hung as though it belonged to someone else. Pain shot down my side.

"Get back in that Jeep, boy!"

Henry paused. His eyes shot over, and I shook my head. Somehow, I managed to sit, dig my heels into the snow for balance, and push my back against a tire. My shoulder burned, and as I shifted my body, another jolt of pain rushed down my side.

"You hurt him!" Henry yelled after seeing me cradle my lifeless arm. "Why'd you have to hurt him? He hasn't done shit to you!"

Mr. Frank swatted the air and shouted, "I didn't hurt him. But if he doesn't stay away from my daughter, I will!"

The threat sickened me. My teeth clacked together. My heart raced. When I looked up at Mr. Frank, there was a glassiness in his eyes I had never seen before, and it haunted me for days. Aggi's dad had changed. He was no longer someone I knew and could trust. That made me angry.

"What time did you say your friend's party started?" Henry asks Jen, and I remember the roof. Aggi.

"Uh . . . I forgot something." I run back toward the stairs, and Jen protests. "Sorry," I call over my shoulder. "I can't leave yet!"

"Well, I can't leave you guys in here after hours, even with your ID. I'll lose my job."

"Come on, Max!" Henry shouts, and I stop. "We'll figure it out."

I drop my head and shuffle back toward Jen and Henry.

Jen says to Henry. "I'll text you my friend's address."

Henry scrambles for his phone and their fingers tap-dance on the screens.

"It starts at ten, but that really means ten thirty or eleven."

Jen's eyes lock onto Henry as she slides her phone into her pocket, and I suddenly feel like the third wheel.

"So, what happened to your face?" She brushes her nose with her knuckle. "It looks painful."

Henry pauses, and I drape my arm across his shoulder. "Henry didn't tell you? He's an MMA fighter."

"Uh . . . no . . . I . . ."

"Oh, Henry." I shake my head. "Always so humble."

Jen tilts her head. "Mixed martial arts, huh?"

Henry shrugs, stares at his feet.

"One of the best in the state." I continue my fib. "Should see the other guy. I mean, guys."

Henry's laugh is contagious.

"Well, see you soon, MMA." Jen motions toward the door, and we stroll onto the sidewalk.

"Wait!" Henry shouts as Jen double-checks the security of the locked door. He's holding his hand in the air. "I fight, but not like that. Not MMA, and not because I want to."

Jen tilts her head, and I squeeze Henry's shoulder. "My brothers are pricks, and sometimes it's better to stay and take it than run and hide." Henry clears his throat.

"It's always two against one," I say. "They're twins and never leave each other's side, though they should. They're poor influences on each other."

"My dad . . . he thinks fighting solves problems."

Jen's eyebrow lifts as she nods.

Henry rubs the bruise on his nose. "This. This is because I wanted the last piece of bacon. I mean, look at me. I'm twice their size." Henry shrugs. "Well, you've never seen my brothers, but they're a lot smaller than me."

Jen smiles and Henry continues.

"They started whining, as they do, and my dad sent us outside to resolve our issues. It was a damn piece of bacon, which

I'd already chewed and swallowed. Get over it! But no . . . we had to go outside and fight. Winner gets what exactly? Me to regurgitate the bacon?" Henry shakes his head. "Sometimes they make no damn sense, especially when they've been drinking."

There is a long pause. Henry rubs his forehead and stares out over the dark campus lit by streetlights. Henry's never shared intimate details behind the fights, and I realize now that my best friend knows more about me than I know about him.

Jen sighs and mumbles, "Toxic masculinity is a real fucked-up thing."

Another pause that seems to drag on forever until Henry stuffs his hands in his pockets, rocks on his heels, and smiles at Jen. A wide, infectious smile.

"I'll see you soon, then?" Jen hesitates before stepping backward.

"You sure will!" Henry shouts, his lips now the shape of a crescent moon.

I shuffle my feet on the sidewalk, while Henry won't stop grinning as Jen disappears onto campus. Henry and I wander back to where we started. Aggi, somewhere on the roof. Me, keeping my distance from her, as I've been told by too many people to do. The frustration overcomes me.

"We have to find Aggi!"

Henry snaps his head. "Oh, shit! Sorry, Max. I don't know what the hell just happened."

I shake my head. "No need to be sorry."

"But I forgot all about Aggi and Umé. I mean, what the hell just happened?" He bends over, grips his knees, and draws deep breaths.

"You're going to have a good night, my friend." I pat Henry's back. "A very good night indeed."

Henry straightens, his stance tight. "You're going with me, right?"

I laugh. "No way. This is *your* night. But send Umé a text and see if they're still here. Before you go, I mean."

On cue, the door of the science building swings open and Grace barrels onto the sidewalk. Out of habit, I spin around, searching for a spot to hide. My chest tightens as I dart behind a row of leafless shrubs.

I can't. She can't.

But what if she did? What if I did?

"I won't knowingly leave you two on the roof." Dr. Nelson says. *What's she doing here?*

"It's not like you'd get fired," Umé says. "You're tenured."

They're walking fast. They have to pass Henry, standing like a streetlight with his back to the building, typing on his phone. Does he even hear them? For sure they will see him and know I'm here, too.

"Grace!" Dr. Nelson shouts. "Come on, honey."

Grace missiles across the grass, aiming in my direction. I tighten my muscles, draw myself into a smaller shape, but she's shouting, and Henry's turning, and . . .

"Hey, Gracie!" Henry says, sliding his phone into his pocket.

"Henry? What are you doing here?" Aggi meets up with Henry, and the two stand directly in front of the bare bushes I'm crouching behind.

"Oh . . . um . . . well . . ." Henry stammers his words.

Umé jogs toward them, holding her hands up and shouting, "It's not what it looks like!"

Her words, the night, seeing Henry fall hard for a girl he just met, nudge me to stand and show Aggi I'm here, too. If Henry would just step to the side. If Aggi would just look over. If she'd . . .

"Why are you hiding in the bushes, Max?" Grace asks.

"Max?" I'm not sure who says my name the second time, but my heart hopes it's Aggi. I crawl out of the bushes, and slink onto the sidewalk, and the campus quiets.

This place belonged to Aggi and me. This is where we were when we lost everything.

Aggi approaches, staring at me. Cheeks flushed from the cold air. Her nose matching the color of her lips. How could she have grown more beautiful since the last time I saw her, which was what? Only hours ago? But the dock doesn't count.

"Grace!" Dr. Nelson shouts, but I steady my gaze. I don't want to look away from her face. "See you tomorrow, Aggi," Dr. Nelson calls out again. "Grace! GRACE! I have a date with Ben and Jerry and a pillow that goes by the name of Benedict Cumberbatch! Now come on, honey!"

I'm magnetized. Two feet in front of Aggi and I can't move. If we stretched out our arms, our fingers would touch. She's frozen, too.

"Max?"

24

"AGGI."

"Why are you in the bushes? And why are you here?"

"I . . . I wanted to see you."

I break my gaze with Max to look over my shoulder. A familiar habit. My dad's voice from that night starting to play in my ear. *Why didn't you pick up? Why didn't you answer?* I was fine on the roof. I didn't hear his words. But now my father's voice is all I hear and it stings, almost as bad as the blame in his eyes.

Grace and Dr. Nelson stroll along the sidewalk heading for the parking lot, but Henry and Umé stand off in the distance like two guardian angels. Henry behind Max, Umé behind me. Our best friends wanting a reunion so badly that it's obvious they planned this. The oversized flakes fall onto

Max's bangs, one melts into his lashes, and he blinks. I want to reach out and brush his hair, but I tuck my hand deep into my pocket.

Max clears his throat and opens his mouth to talk, but as soon as he begins, the campus bells chime from the tower. Nine slow tolls. By the time the bells stop ringing, Henry and Umé have joined us.

"We're sorry," Umé says.

"It's just that—" Henry begins, but Max grabs his shoulder.

"I wanted to see you," Max blurts. "I wanted to see if Grace was okay after falling in the lake. And I needed to see that you're okay, too."

I don't know how to answer.

"Aggi!" Dr. Nelson shouts from the parking lot. "Shoot me a text when you get home tonight!"

I wave to let her know I heard.

"We need to go," I say, turning from Max. I want to talk to him and tell him I'm not okay, that I haven't been since the accident, but there is a risk of my dad waking up and wondering where I am. He's looked for me before and he could do it again.

"Wait!" Max calls, but I keep walking. I refuse to turn around.

25

MAX

"AGGI?"

I've called her name three times, but she won't turn around. Umé locks arms with her as they follow the sidewalk toward the parking lot.

"Henry?" I whisper as he drapes his arm over me.

"Give her space," he says. "I don't think she's ready."

The snowflakes, fluffier now, sugarcoat the back of Aggi's hair. The sidewalk distances between us as my feet slide slowly across the path. At the fork, Aggi and Umé hesitate, hushing their voices when Henry and I pass. Aggi needs more space, more time, commodities I seem to never run out of, yet it always feels like I don't have enough. I want to believe I'll wait for as long as it takes, as long as Aggi needs, but even forever seems so short. A year ago I lost my brother, Kate, Aggi. But it feels like they left me yesterday, an hour ago, a minute . . .

Henry calls out to Umé, and the two meet on the sidewalk, probably planning another fruitless reunion. I shuffle toward Henry's truck, glancing back at Aggi ten thousand times. She looks at me once, but it's that single stare that heats me from the inside out.

Standing beside Henry's truck, snow turning my black hair white, I watch the girl I've loved my whole life climb into her friend's car and turn her back to me. As she slams the door, I wave. I don't know if she sees me, or even if I'm waving at her or only a memory of her. My wave seems more final. A farewell to us.

When Henry jogs over, saying, "It's already nine o'clock," I still don't move.

The urge to stare at Aggi's silhouette in the car window prevents me from budging. I'm frozen with the finality of losing everyone I've ever loved. I stare at the glass until Henry shouts, "Get in, Max! By the time we find this party, it'll be ten."

The last thing I want to do is be a high school student at a college party wearing someone's too-big-for-me shoes. I'd rather go home and watch television with my parents. Eat popcorn and stare at the screen while they laugh and disengage. But my mind fights against itself as it searches for answers only Aggi can explain. *What happened to us? Why did we let our dads come between us? Do you blame me like your father does?* And then: *I'm sorry. If I could rewind the clock, I'd insist you answer the phone that night. Blame me, not yourself. I do.*

For weeks after Kate died, I followed Aggi to work, to school, wondering if she was okay. I wasn't sure of my own brokenness—I barely held my shit together—but somehow following Aggi made me feel less fractured. I sent her texts in the middle of the night—too many to count—until they stopped going through. My calls shot straight to voice mail. My knocks went unanswered. Then her father threatened me, my dad; and I promised my parents I'd stop pushing for answers. I never gave up hope, though, until now.

Henry's still rambling about Jen, pausing to interject apologies about how it went with Aggi. I nod, my eyes fixed on Umé's car, and I drop my head against the window as Henry turns the key.

Click.

Click.

Click.

At the same time, we remember the lights.

"No! No! No!" Henry punches the steering wheel, and the horn wails.

"Shit! Shit! Shit!"

"This is not happening right now!" Henry slaps the seat.

"I'm afraid it is," I mumble.

Henry jumps out of the truck, waving his arms, then leaning back into the cab and pushing the horn. "Umé! Umé!" He grabs his phone while I sit worthless in the seat and do

175

nothing, and within seconds Umé and Aggi are parked at the back of Henry's truck.

In the side mirror, my eyes fall on Aggi's shadow. Hands wave. Aggi tears her hat from her head and yanks at her hair. Are they arguing?

Umé's car door opens. "Won't start, huh?"

"Dead battery," Henry says. "We left the lights on." Henry glances at me, and I shrug.

"Jumper cables are in my trunk," Umé says. "But I don't think they'll reach. Why'd you park next to a giant snowbank?"

Henry pushes the button on his phone to check the time.

"I need to be somewhere. Can you just give us a ride?"

"No!" I snap, and climb out of the truck. I shuffle over to Henry and Umé, and Umé stares at my feet.

"Why are you walking like that?"

"Like what?"

She tips her head toward my feet. "I can take you to Max's. You probably have jumper cables in the Jeep, right? But I'd have to drop Aggi off at my house. Logistics, you know."

How could I forget? If Aggi's dad, or my dad for that matter, saw Aggi and me riding in the same car, it would complicate tonight even more.

I fidget, unsure what to do with my hands, as I glance at Aggi statue-like in the car. She's close again. The window near enough to touch.

"Look," Henry says. "We're on our way to a party. If you

can't take us, we'll walk, but if we freeze to death—Umé—it's on your damn conscience."

Umé huffs and motions Henry toward the trunk. They powwow for a minute while I stuff my hands into my pockets and skate around the bed of Henry's pickup. I wonder if a sudden movement, me sprinting or sliding past Aggi's window, would make her head turn.

I consider leaping on the ice, doing something ridiculous that will make her laugh—I could always make her laugh but had to earn it—then I remember how she looked at me on the sidewalk before turning away.

Umé snaps, "Okay! Get in the damn car before we turn to ice."

I don't budge. Unless Aggi looks over at me, offers a nudge, signals it's okay for me to climb into the same car she's riding in, I'm going nowhere. She doesn't want me near her and I have to repect that.

Henry slides into the back seat and I continue to stand in the snow as a slide show of my life flashes before me. Aggi, chasing after me into the woods, shouting, "Max, Max, where are you hiding?" We are no more than seven years old. Aggi squealing as I dart behind a tree, then yelping as she trips and knocks her knee on a rock. She's crying, and I'm racing home to get the rusty red wheelbarrow we keep in the barn. I'm flying between the trees, jumping over logs, moving at a speed I've never reached before. As I struggle to push the wheelbarrow back to where Aggi fell, I stop to line the bottom with pine straw. I lift Aggi with superhuman seven-year-old strength and spill her from my arms onto the cushioned wheelbarrow bed. Today, I still don't know how I lifted Aggi or the wheelbarrow. I don't remember how I navigated the woods and brought her home. But my noodle arms and knobby knees took Aggi to safety. She was bleeding. She needed help. After Aggi returned home from the doctor, seven stitches later, I stopped by her house to check on her. She kissed the top of my head and said, "You're so strong, Maxwell Granger. You're the strongest boy I know."

"Dammit, Max!" Aggi shouts. "Get in this car before you freeze to death."

My chest constricts. This can't be happening. Aggi, commanding I get into the car. I pinch the bridge of my nose and flick a tear from my cheek. Strongest boy, my ass.

26

HOT PUFFS OF AIR HIT my neck every three seconds. I sniff, hoping to detect a hint of peppermint or Tic Tacs, but I'm also concentrating on keeping my own mouth closed so I don't flood the car with bacon breath. Lucio & Sons' BLT pizza lingers in your mouth for days, no matter how many mints you pop, and I had no time to pop one before I yelled at Max to get into the car.

"Turn here." Henry hits the back of Umé's seat, and Umé cranks the wheel. Our bodies tilt.

"A little notice next time would be great," Umé snaps.

"Sorry. I don't know this part of town."

I fumble with the heater, adjusting it to blow stronger on the back seat. Max is likely cold.

"This should be the street," Henry says. "A few more houses down on the right."

"A college party, huh?" Umé says. "You sure you're invited?"

Henry laughs. "Most definitely invited."

"By a girl named Jen," Max says, and I hold my breath.

"By a *woman* named Jen," Henry corrects.

"Do tell more," Umé says. "This Jen's in college?"

"She works campus security, too," Henry says. "Could she be any more amazing?"

Cars line the curb, packed so tightly no one's going to be able to leave. Umé slows in front of a duplex where two shabby recliners sit on a front porch.

"This is it!" Henry shouts.

I grab the *oh, shit* handle on the roof as Umé whips into the driveway, slams the car into reverse, and backs up.

"Where are you going?" Henry snaps. "Just let us out here."

"Settle it, Henry. I'm not getting wedged in like the rest of these drunks." Umé parallel parks between a dumpster and a car buried by a snowplow, and cuts the engine.

"We're coming with you," Umé says, smiling at me. "This definitely looks like the place to be, and Aggi and I don't have any plans . . . Right, Aggi?"

Umé and Henry make eye contact in the mirror, and I pretend not to notice. Another plan our best friends contrive to get Max and me alone. I sink deeper into the seat, and Max's knee drives into my back as he shifts and climbs from the car. It's the tightest space we've been in together for months. Aside from Max grabbing my ass in the lake, we haven't

180

touched each other, either, which reminds me that I really should thank him for helping me with Grace.

"No plans," Umé repeats. "Right, Aggi?" She seems to be speaking in slow motion.

My eyes fixate on Max, his hand, opening my door. Why is he doing that? Now's not the time for his Southern gentleman charm. But maybe now is the time for me to say thank you.

Max stares at the ground as I climb from the car. I am close enough to see his chapped lips and dimples. My arm brushes his coat. I want to scream.

His head lifts as I move beside him. "Hi," he whispers, and closes his eyes.

This is not a good idea, the voice in my head shouts. *Go home! Get out of here, before Dad catches you with him!* I try to silence the words that cement my legs to the ground, but Max, Henry, Umé, all watch with eager eyes. Well, Max is back to staring at his feet and those ridiculously oversized shoes he's wearing.

Henry pushes Max toward the sidewalk, and Umé says, "Come on. This is going to be good for you."

I shake my head. "This is not a good idea." Max and Henry reach the front door and Max turns. "This is, in fact, the worst possible idea ever," I say.

"Partying with college kids," Umé says. "What could possibly go wrong?"

At the front door, the bass rattles the windows. Umé grabs my hand and shouts to be heard, "Will you promise to at least talk to him? Nobody here knows you! No one will find out!"

Umé's words flutter in my mind and believing them is dangerous. Even if I'm among a sea of strangers, my father's ears burn. After Kate died and the attorneys fueled my father's paranoia, he started questioning my every move. Where was I going? Who was I with? Myself, bound by fear, I let my dad shackle me and keep me from the boy I love. Max embodies freedom to my father, which scares him after he's lost one child. How can he lose another? But he doesn't understand that by shutting everyone out, by turning his back on the people he once loved, he's destroying the family he has left. Max didn't hurt our family. Max and his parents aren't to blame. But Dad refuses to hear the truth. He loves his anger more than he loves his family.

Stopping at the door, Umé and I stare at each other. "Do we knock?" I ask.

Umé shrugs. "What did Max and Henry do? Why didn't they wait for us?"

I didn't see Max or Henry go in, and I'm unsure what we should do now. I've never been to a college party, only lake-kid parties where we sit on docks, build bonfires, throw Frisbees, and swim. Nothing's preplanned and organized. We simply show up to an outdoor space and call it a party. After Connor moved to the lake, we started getting invites to *get-togethers* and *cookout brunches*, and Max complained a lot about Connor trying too hard to fit in, but we always went. We loved seeing the lake through a different lens.

"What if we were supposed to bring beer?" Umé asks.

My face scrunches. "Isn't there a rule that if you drink you should bring something? We just won't drink."

Umé nods in full agreement.

I punch the doorbell as a car pulls up at the curb and out pile four girls and a guy. We back up as they push for the door, and follow into the house behind them like we're part of their squad.

Umé palms my back. "It's so dark in here!"

The foyer—all four feet of it—dumps into a crowded living room. Shoulders bump shoulders as we slide through the crowd. I glimpse Henry weaving around warm bodies in search of the campus security girl. Jen sounds great, and I'm excited to meet her. I already picture her standing six inches taller than Henry. Henry has height criteria that must be met. He likes tall, muscular, or meaty girls—the reason he was attracted to Umé until she made it quite clear they weren't compatible. Henry's always been into girls who could potentially kick his ass (his words) but would never, ever, in a million years do so.

A guy twists in front of me and elbows my boob.

"Excuse me!" I snap, and he whips around.

"Can I help you?" he asks, scanning me head to toe.

I scrunch my nose and squeeze through the crowded room in search of someplace to sit. When I reach a sofa, I plop onto the rust-colored cushion and catch a glimpse of Umé on the other side of the room.

She shouts, "You going to be okay?" and I shoot a thumbs-up. "I'll be right here in the kitchen!" She points to a connecting room.

The girl next to me smiles. "Weed's in the basement."

My eyes widen—an obvious sign that I am not in college—but I nod to assure her I'm fully aware of the weed location. What I want to say is that the weed is everywhere. The air thick with the distinct skunk smell.

My phone vibrates in my hand with a text from Henry.

I swipe the screen. *Would you meet me in the basement? X*

My heart revs, and I read the message again. It's not from Henry. X is Max. He's been X since we were kids. I've been O since our first kiss.

I send a text to Umé. *Max is texting me from Henry's phone. Are you aware?*

Umé: *Yep.*

Me: *Why?*

Umé: *He can't use his phone. Your dad, remember?*

I frantically type. *My dad will check MY phone. Remember?*

Umé: *Just go to the basement! NOW!!! Then delete all texts.*

I groan, and the girl next to me asks if I'm okay. A quick nod, and I say, "I really need to get to the basement."

She smiles sympathetically. "Second door on the right."

Meeting Max in a dark basement filled with marijuana smoke isn't exactly the picture of romance, but love leads you through darkness, or a dark smoke-filled basement, walls lined with drunk and lip-locked college students. *Everything*

184

will be fine, I tell myself. *Dad will never know.* It's not like I'm planning to run away with Max; we're only going to talk. I'm going to say, *Thank you, Max, for helping rescue Grace.* I'd be the world's biggest asshole if I didn't at least do that.

As I walk down the stairs toward the basement, the pungent smoke makes my eyes water. Can you be allergic to weed?

In the basement, it takes a moment for my eyes to adjust to the dim light and thick haze. I glance around the room for Max and glimpse Henry talking to a gorgeous girl I assume is Jen. She matches Henry in height, which makes me smile. Henry reaches toward her and picks lint from her shoulder, and she collects his hand in hers and yanks him toward her. *Way to go, Henry.*

There's Umé cornering the stairwell and strutting over to a table. She plops on top and crosses her legs. A guy and girl turn toward her and laugh at something she says. No matter the setting, Umé fits like the missing puzzle piece.

I scoop my hair across one shoulder, draw a deep breath, and try not to cough. Max, standing on the other side of the room, leans against the back of an empty chair. He's rubbing his neck, back, shoulder, arm. I can hardly keep track of Max's hands. They fidget until his eyes land on me, and all movement in the room stops.

I step forward, and Max matches my move. The voices wind up in my head and prevent a second step. *He probably blames you like his family does.* But if he did, would he have sent me that text? *He's been seeing other girls. He's just going to tell you to move on*. But I need to thank him, and if I don't do it now, there may not be another opportunity. *You're using Grace as an excuse.*

"So what?" I murmur, and step forward.

Tonight I actually have an excuse to talk to Max. Six months may pass before another excuse presents itself, and I can't even think of what could happen to us during that time. If I go home now, I'll sit in my room all night thinking on what I should have done. Max jumped into the lake without hesitation. He didn't think; he reacted. He ordered the guys on the dock to make sure we were okay. Max wasn't putting on a show. I know him better than that.

As if a giant robot hand picks me up in its metal claw by the back of the shirt and carries me over to Max, suddenly I'm in front of him. I don't remember the walk, sidestepping the crowd of college kids, but here I am, six inches from him, saying, "Hey."

"Hey." His response is breathy, and his warm eyes make me tremble with excitement, and also with fear that someone will see me. Someone who knows my dad. Someone who knows what I'm feeling. "Thanks for meeting me here," he says, and my throat catches.

The urge to grab Max and kiss him comes out of nowhere.

"Thank you," I whisper.

He leans forward. "I'm sorry. What?"

"Thank you," I repeat, though I think his question was an excuse to move closer.

His eyebrows arch, cheekbones surface. "For what?"

"What you did for Grace. You know, helping to find her."

We smile at the same time; then our chins drop and we stare at our feet, unsure how to navigate this awkward moment. Suddenly, I'm aware of the music in the room, louder than before. And it's a song Cal used to play on his guitar. One Kate used to sing. I glance at Max. He raises his chin and our eyes lock.

"You don't have to——"

"What?"

"Huh?"

"I want to—"

Max leans toward my face, and I think he's going to kiss me. I'm unsure how to feel about it, except—maybe—I want him to?

His voice. The hazy room. Guitar chords.

Instinctively, I shut my eyes.

27

AGGI SHUTS HER EYES, AND I don't know what to do. The music and voices make it impossible to hear her. Did she ask me to kiss her? I lean closer, and for a moment I think: *Maybe? Should I?* But this is all happening so fast. Then instinct takes over, and I'm cupping her cheek.

Aggi's eyes pop open then quickly shut, and I draw a deep breath.

"No need to thank me," I shout in Aggi's ear, and her eyes snap open again. "I wish I'd been sitting on the dock with her and stopped it from happening."

"The dock?" Aggi tilts her head. "Yeah. The dock."

She smiles, and her eyes widen. I'm still holding her cheek, refusing to let go, and she's leaning her head into my hand like it's a pillow. My insides twist into knots as memories of us together zigzag through my mind. We're on my porch bouncing a rubber ball between us while Pawtrick Swayze weaves in and out of our legs. We're at the lake laughing while Henry and I perfect our belly flops off the dock. We're on the rooftop of the science building, our lips wet with want as our bodies join for the first time. If I don't kiss Aggi right now . . . But I need to ask her first. We haven't been together in months, and I haven't a clue if spontaneity is a part of us anymore. It's our thousandth kiss, but it feels like the first.

"Aggi?"

"Yeah?"

I slide my fingers into the hair above her ear and sigh. She closes her eyes again, and as I'm about to ask if it's okay to kiss her, the song changes to something drum-heavy, and I jump.

"Ouch!"

28

Aggi

MAX YANKS MY HAIR, PRACTICALLY ripping it from my scalp.

"My bracelet's stuck!"

"Your what?"

"My bracelet."

Since when does Max wear a bracelet?

"Can you stop pulling my hair?" Max won't relent. He's twisting my curls around his wrist.

"I'm really sorry, but can you hold still?"

"That's so painful. Please stop yanking my hair."

"I'm so sorry! I can't unwind my hand. The beads are stuck."

I grab his wrist and pull at the strand of hair twisted around the wooden beads. Max's hand smacks my ear.

"God. Sorry!" Max says.

"It won't budge."

"I'll take it off." Max's fingers, warm against my scalp, poke and prod around my head. His touch, even the jabs, charges every cell in my body. My muscles bubble with memory, reminded of the last time we were this close.

That night, on top of the science building, on top of each other. Sure, it was a bumbling first time, but it was *our* first time, and we've never had a second. The thrill of the memory coils with pain and guilt. We were messing around while Kate's car was hitting black ice. We were pawing and panting with want, spinning out of control while Cal struggled for his life. We could barely breathe while Max's brother took his last breath.

Max slips out of his bracelet, leaving the wooden beads dangling in my hair. "We'll probably need to cut it out."

We'll. There's no "we" anymore. There can't be.

"Thanks, but I'll manage." I stress the word "I'll" to smother his "we'll."

Max rubs the back of his neck.

"Well . . . thanks."

Guilt has found me again, choking out the words I'd like to say to Max. I want to tell him what I'm feeling, and I want to hear what he's feeling, too, but I'm afraid someone will see us and Dad will find out Max and I were alone together. He'll think we planned it. He'll accuse me of not caring about Kate. How I'm to blame for the accident. If Max and I hadn't been on the roof that night—if we'd been anywhere but there—my sister, his brother, would still be alive.

"Max?" I say his name with urgency. Guilt ferries me to unanswered questions. I want to know if he blames me like

191

my father does, as it was my idea to go to the science building that night.

Max eyeballs the beads in my hair. "You don't have to thank me, Aggi. Grace is like a sister."

Max, the way he says my name, the way he thinks of Grace as family, the way his head bobbles when he talks, buckles my knees beneath me. I wobble, but is it the sound of his voice or the herb-tinted air? I've been downstairs sucking second-hand smoke for many minutes, and now I'm light-headed—in fact, my whole body feels like it might lift and float like a helium-filled balloon.

Maybe it's the smoke or the song playing its love-locked chorus on a wheel. Maybe it's that Max and I haven't touched each other since the night that tore us apart. Whatever it is, I can't bring myself to look away from his face. My eyes lock onto his nose, cheeks, lips. My heart focuses on the likelihood that I'm going to kiss him and then walk away like nothing ever happened. There are too many questions, and I'm afraid of the answers. I'd rather feel the press of his lips against mine, even if it is the last time. That urgent swipe and push as our lips find each other again. How our mouths split apart and tongues wrap and intertwine.

I have to kiss him.

Then I'll leave. Search for Umé and insist we go.

Just one long kiss. One last time. Something to remember him by. It's been so long.

Then I won't look back. Ever.

29

MAX

IF I DON'T KISS AGGI I'm going up in smoke. We can't
leave now without a kiss. This is the first time we've been
alone—in a crowded room—since Cal and Kate died. If Aggi
leaves with me bumbling over my words, saying no more than
"You don't have to thank me," I'll combust and then live with
regret. What if we never get another chance? What if we're
never alone again? Aggi's dad warned me to never speak to
his daughter, but I'll risk my life if it means I'm back in hers.

Aggi and her long blinks and tiny steps back and forth.
She's confused, too. But then she leans in and I match her
move, forcing myself to stare at her face, not my bracelet
stuck in her hair. I hope I'm not misreading the moment, but
I don't think I care anymore. The only thing I care about is
kissing her. A reward that outweighs all risks. And I'm about

to take the risk I've wanted to take for months.

"Aggi?"

"Yeah?"

"Can I—?"

The guy next to me turns, laughs, and blows smoke into my face. I cough and wave away the cloud. Aggi smiles, covering her face with her hands. She's beautiful up close, more beautiful than I remember. Her freckles splash her nose and spill onto her cheeks, her lips lined in a color to match. She slides her hands from her face and parts her lips but not to speak. I step closer, brushing my body against hers.

She grabs my neck and yanks me toward her. *Holy shit!* This is really happening.

30

Aggi

WHEN YOU WANT SOMEONE SO bad every inch of your body aches, you'll stop at nothing to get them. You'll dive into freezing lake waters, shovel already-shoveled snow, sit on the porch and watch for a shadow in the window, long for a wave.

Max needed me like I needed him. We lost two of the most precious people in our lives, and then we lost each other. I joked about having a stalker, and then eventually I bought my dad's lies. Max isn't a fact finder. He's showing all the signs of a boy in love. At least the signs I recognize.

There is only one way to know for sure how Max feels, but first I need him to answer a couple of questions.

I reach around Max's neck and yank him toward me. His back bends forward, his ear at my lips. "What are you trying to accomplish by bringing girls to your house every week?

195

Are you trying to make me jealous?"

Max's eyes widen as his lips tremble and his mouth pops open like a baby bird's. He looks at me, then the floor, the ceiling. He tugs at his shirt.

"Stop fidgeting, Maxwell! I deserve answers! I have to make sense of what you've been doing. Following me around yet seeing other girls."

Baby-bird mouth again. No words except "I . . . I . . . I . . ."

"Following me to work makes sense. Sitting outside my window after you've pretended to shovel the driveway, I get. But you know I'm sitting at my desk watching as you bring a new 'friend' home. If you're doing it to make me jealous, you succeeded!" I feel heat in my cheeks, my breath heavy, annoyance bubbling inside me where affection lingered mere seconds ago. Max has some explaining to do. No matter how bad I want this big, romantic reunion with him, I have to make sense of how he's been acting for months.

Max scratches his cheek, clears his throat. "It's not how it looks. I promise."

"But you shout so the entire woods hears how happy you are. How you have the house to yourself. And every Friday— like clockwork—you bring someone new home. You're never by yourself. Don't you want to be alone, or with . . ." I stop myself and Max sighs.

"If you're trying to make me jealous, that's so unfair." I fold my arms. "Unfair to those girls at your house. Unfair to me. I realize we haven't spoken in almost a year, but I thought

I knew you. Have you really changed that much? I mean, you're even wearing bracelets now!" I flick my hair and the beads jingle at my ear.

Max reaches for the bracelet, leans in, and gently unwinds my hair from the beads. "I thought that's what you wanted," he says at my ear. "For me to leave you alone." He rolls the bracelet between his fingers and draws a deep breath. "This was Cal's, by the way. Sorry it got stuck in your hair."

"You thought it was what *I* wanted?"

"For me to move on. For *us* to move on. So I thought if you saw me with those girls, you'd think I'd moved on."

"Max! I see you everywhere! You're not exactly the best stalker." The word slips, and he winces.

"That's what you think of me? A stalker?" Max's chin drops. He wipes his eye, and I wonder if it's a tear or if the smoke is burning. "I did everything the wrong way, but I didn't know what to do or how to do it. This year, without my brother, without you—I'm just trying to figure out how to survive without the people I love."

The room spins and my heart pounds.

I grab Max's free hand and draw it to my chest as I close my eyes and inch closer to kiss him. I lean in. Max leans in, too. We're so close his hot breath puffs my face. As we inch closer, and closer still, Henry slams into us, shouting, "We have to get out of here now! NOW!"

31

LEAVE IT TO MY BEST friend to interrupt me as my lips are centimeters from Aggi's. Goose bumps cover me, head to toe. A cloud of smoke burns my eyes, yet Aggi is all I see, in focus and sunlight bright. My legs are rubber, ankles melting, and if I'm not mistaken, I quite possibly have a boner.

"No. No! NO!" I shout in Henry's face and he flinches. "Not going. Not going anywhere. I can't." I glance down, then back at Henry. Does he not see the predicament I'm in?

Henry grabs my shirt. "My brothers texted Umé and she told them where we were! They're going to beat my ass for hiding their keys! They've been circling the house in my dad's truck, and we have to get out of here!"

I turn to Aggi. "Go with us?"

She pauses. Worry in her eyes. She has her own devils

messing with her head, and I want to wrestle them to the ground and pummel their faces, but instead I beg, "Please, Aggi. I want to answer all those questions you asked me. One last talk. We owe it to ourselves. To them." Kate and Cal.

Henry comes between us as he shoves me toward the basement stairs. We race toward the back door. In the dim porch light, I'm afraid to turn around and check if Aggi followed.

32

WHAT DOES MAX MEAN BY "one last talk"? After
tonight, will he never speak to me again? Maybe he's hurt by
me calling him a stalker.

I trudge up the stairs behind the boys. Jen is waiting for us
on the landing and grabs Henry's arm, swings the back door
open, and shouts, "Through here!"

I should duck out, find Umé, and insist we leave so I can
avoid this "one last talk." But Max and I may never speak
again, and then I'd be full of regret.

At the doorway, Max leans against a metal pipe railing,
shifting his pants and patting his crotch, and I force myself
to look away. Jen and Henry huddle in the backyard, Henry's
voice wound tight.

"I'm so sorry, but I have to go!" Henry says. "Earlier, I

took my brothers' keys. They were in no condition to drive, and I knew they'd be pissed when they discovered their keys missing. They'd come after me."

"Oh, Henry," Max says from the steps.

Henry clears his throat. "Yeah. Probably shouldn't have done that." He swats the air. "I should have taken their truck, too, and driven it smack-dab into the lake. Because when they find me—"

"Really wish you'd left them alone," Max says, shaking his head.

Henry races to the corner of the house for a peek, and Jen follows.

Max looks back at me and hesitates. I smile.

"Will you please go with us?"

I shake my head. "I can't. . . . I won't leave Umé."

"They're circling around again!" Henry shouts, and plasters himself against the wall of the house. "We have to go!"

Max jumps from the steps, grabs Henry, and says, "Just stand up to them!"

"Hah!"

"I'm serious," Max says. "You're always letting them settle the score the way your dad says to settle it, the way they want to. Why can't they settle it the way you want?"

Jen interrupts. "Why is there a fucking score to settle in the first place? You're brothers."

Henry and Max glance at Jen, neither speaking, only nodding.

The truck slows in front of the house, and Henry peeks around the edge again. "There's Umé! What the hell is she doing?"

I leap from the steps and trail Max and Jen to the corner of the house. The truck is stopped, window down, and Umé's pointing toward the front steps as if she's telling them Henry's inside the house.

"I hope she's not doing what I think she is!" Henry says.

"Did you tell her you'd taken their keys?" Max asks.

"Didn't get a chance to explain after she told me they texted her. I was too busy freaking out that she'd told them where we were!"

Jen aims her key fob at a black Honda parked on the opposite side of the street. She says, "Tuck your coat over your head and run to my car!" She tosses Henry her keys. "You drive! I had a beer."

"We're going with you," Max says, and reaches for my hand.

I pause as Henry pulls his coat over his head. Max's eyes urge me to go, to take hold of his hand. My chest tightens. I know I shouldn't, but Henry's counting to three and Jen's shouting, "Let's go!"

As Henry's brothers pull away from the curb, we sprint— all four of us—across the street. Max's door won't open and Henry frantically pushes buttons on the key fob. The beep-beep draws Umé's eyes to us and she shouts, "Hey! Where are you guys going?"

"Get in!" Henry screams, and we dive into the car.

Henry slams on the gas and we fishtail down the road, heading in the opposite direction of the twins.

When I slip my phone from my coat to text Umé and fill her in on what the hell is going on, my stomach turns to knots. Two messages from my dad. I refuse to check them, which sickens me even more, but I send a vague text to Umé that reads: *Call me*. Additional details would get me into more trouble than I'm already in.

I don't know where we're going or why I chose to go. The spontaneity feels good, though, and for the first time in months I feel taking a risk is exactly what I need to do. I am having fun again.

33

MAX

AGGI AND I END UP in the back seat of Jen's Honda, me pushed into the passenger-side door and Aggi perched in the middle. She has yet to slide back over to her side, and I'm not complaining. Her knee bumps mine and presses into my thigh as I straighten my back. The courage I felt in the dark, smoke-filled basement fades. In the car, the air's clear and smells of peppermint, the streetlights shine on us like spotlights, and I've never felt so vulnerable.

Jen flips around in her seat as Henry runs a stop sign. "That was your friend, right, talking to Henry's brothers?"

Aggi glances at her phone screen, and I glimpse a text from her dad. "Yeah. I just texted her." She swipes the unread text bubble into oblivion. "Haven't heard from her yet. She probably thinks we left her."

"We did," I mumble, and grit my teeth when Aggi glances over.

"I saw her on the porch earlier talking to a girl," Jen says. I think she's trying to put Aggi's mind at ease. She senses Aggi's worried about her friend, but I know her concerns run deeper.

Henry taps the gas and turns the corner.

"Where do you plan on going?" I ask, and Henry glances in the rearview mirror. "They already know you're in town. At a party." We skid as he approaches a stop sign.

"I'm not taking any chances, especially now that Umé clearly told them we were inside."

"I though you hid their spare set of keys."

Henry ignores me and revs the engine, squinting down the cross street. "Aggi?" he says. "Text Umé again and see what they told her."

Aggi scoots forward. "I already did and haven't heard back."

Headlights shine from an approaching vehicle, and as the truck draws closer, Henry slams the gas pedal and we fishtail across the street. "Hold on!" Henry shouts.

Aggi slams back into the seat and slides sideways against my shoulder.

"A little easier on my car, please," Jen says, and Henry flashes a sheepish grin.

"Sorry. I thought it was my brothers."

Aggi takes her time removing herself from my shoulder. "Oops," she mumbles.

But I hear "sorry" and say, "Oh, no. You don't have to be sorry." Her eyebrow lifts, and I realize Henry's the one who apologized.

"So why are we running from your brothers this time?" Aggi asks, and hearing the word "we" feels wonderful and makes me smile.

We've done this before—Aggi, Henry, Umé, and me—a couple of summers ago, when Henry's brothers found his Hawaii fund and stole forty bucks. Henry was furious. He'd worked hard for that money, selling eggs and in-season fruit at the farmers market as his mother had done before Henry was born. Henry drove fifty miles every weekend to sell goods, and he never missed a day unless Mr. Parker, the farmer Henry worked for, called to tell him he couldn't afford to pay him that week.

"Why can't you tell your dad what your brothers did?" I'd ask, but Henry would shake his head and insist that his father was as trustworthy as the twins and would likely steal the rest of Henry's money and spend it on beer. Henry took matters into his own hands. He lives in a house of adversaries. If taking the twins' keys earns him back a moment of power, I don't blame him one bit.

Henry doesn't always fill me in on the details of his life, but they're not difficult to figure out when he shows up at school with rug burn on his cheekbones or a gash on the bridge of his nose. Henry says that his brothers are angry over the way their lives turned out, and he's probably right. What I don't get is why Henry refuses to fight back.

His brothers don't argue and then laugh it off the way Cal and I did. Henry can't tell his father he's being picked on by the twins, because Henry's a mountain and his twin brothers are anthills. The sheer difference in size causes Henry's father to side with the twins. But Henry's the underdog. It's two—three if you count Henry's father—against one. They outnumber him. And Henry refuses to stick up for himself. "They're my brothers, Max. I won't hit my brother."

When the twins were younger, they used to trap stray cats and cage them up in their backyard without food or water. Henry would show up on my porch in the middle of the night with a patchy-furred bag of bones and ask me if we had milk. We'd sit in the backyard swatting mosquitoes and take turns nursing the stray back to health. I'd listen as Henry shared details of his rescue mission and how he'd snuck out of his trailer to save a caged cat. His brothers quit tormenting cats years ago, but now I fear Henry has become the cat.

Henry's too focused on the road, squinting at headlights, to respond to Aggi's question. "Henry took their keys," I say. "Long story."

Aggi smiles, and I wonder if she's remembering the times we raced through the woods on foot or in the Jeep, trying to outwit Henry's brothers.

"We should drive to the barn," Aggi says, and we lock eyes. She does remember. "They've never found us there before."

"You're brilliant!" Henry shouts, then steadies his voice. "But what about your dad? What about Max's?"

Aggi shifts in her seat. "We're in Jen's car. We can cut the lights and creep into the barn. Once we're inside . . ." She exhales.

She's worried, and now I am, too. Getting this close to our houses, while we're together, could be disastrous.

I drop my head in Aggi's direction and watch as she types a text message. She catches me staring and peeks out of the corner of her eye. "Letting Umé know where we'll be," she whispers.

I hesitate, my heart pounding in my chest. "I never answered your questions," I whisper back. "And I'd like to."

She tilts her head, and I lean so close I can hear her swallow.

Henry and Jen chat about music, which signals that Henry is relaxing now that we have a plan in place. He's grinning as Jen describes how Henry reminds her of some character on some show Henry will most certainly have me Google when we're back at my house late tonight.

Aggi's staring at the floorboard now, her hands tucked in her lap as she squeezes her phone. She has yet to respond to my words.

I sigh and she inhales. Then she blows the air out with force, turns to me, and slaps my leg. I jump.

"Look. You said we needed to have one last talk. Tonight, right?"

Did I say that? One last talk. It suddenly sounds finite. Not at all what I intended.

"No . . . ," I say, and stop. "I thought you were worried about your dad finding out we're together. Tonight, I mean. Not together, just . . ." *Shut up, Max.*

Aggi sighs again. "But you said you wanted to talk. One last time. And I think you're right. We should."

I could kick myself for my choice of words. I didn't mean one last time, but that's what I said, and Aggi thinks it's a good idea now, so I guess I said something right for a change, though she emphasized the words "one last time."

"Yeah," I whisper, sliding against the door, adding distance between us. "One. Last. Time."

34

Aggi

I'M HAVING SERIOUS SECOND THOUGHTS about being here. I should be at the party with Umé. I should be home in bed. One moment Max looks at me like he used to, the next he's recoiling and plastering his shoulder to the car door, drawing as far away from me as he can. He's not making sense. And why am I sitting so close to him? Though I refuse to move away.

We're on the highway heading back to Walabash Woods. Henry's and Jen's voices have lowered, and Jen's leaning across the console, tracing the back of Henry's hand with her nails. Max sighs, and I glance over, dropping my hand non-chalantly on the seat. What am I doing? My mind splits in two, but my body is clear on how to respond when Max and I are alone in the back seat. Physically, I pull toward Max, but the closer we get to the lake, the more fear stops me from going the distance.

Maybe Max blames me like my dad said he did. Maybe Max regrets what happened between us. If we hadn't fallen in love, my sister, his brother, wouldn't be dead.

I fold my hands and bring them to my mouth. The heater blasts on my face, and I slump to the side to avoid the hot air. When I shift my weight, Max glances over and I quickly look out the window. I think I hear him sigh.

"Can we stop somewhere?" Max asks Henry. "I need some . . . air."

35

MAX

"AIR" IS CODE FOR *I need to talk to Henry.*

There are no truck stops, no convenience stores, for miles. Plum Lake Café is ten miles north, and the town we just left is five miles behind us. Henry pulls off onto the nearest private road and parks.

"Here we go," Henry says. "Fresh air."

I tap Henry on the shoulder and insist he come with me.

"But it's cold out there." I tug at his coat, and he groans. "We'll be right back," he says, closing the door.

We walk along the grated road, stepping over frozen slush the snowplow missed.

"I'm not standing with you while you piss." Henry stops near a locked metal gate.

"I don't have to piss. I just really needed to talk to you."

Henry kicks a chunk of snow and I stuff my hands into my coat pockets. We turn our backs to the headlights. I clear my throat and let my worries fly.

"Aggi's dad said he'd kill me if I ever spoke to her again, and here I am. Arms wide. Ready to beckon death. What the hell am I doing?"

Henry taps his heel on a layer of ice, chipping it into shards. "Who cares what Aggi's dad said? You still love her, right?"

The darkness conceals the tears in my eyes when I look at Henry, in the beam of the headlights, and say, "I never stopped."

Henry slugs my arm. "So why fight it?"

"But her dad. My own dad. God, Henry, I'm so scared."

Henry spins around and kicks a pile of snow. The breeze blows flakes back in our faces. "Fuck her dad!" Henry shouts. "Fuck everyone who thinks they can run your life and turn it into something they want it to be. You're in charge of you, Max. Aggi's dad isn't yours. He can tell you to stay away from Aggi all he wants, but he can't force you to do it." Henry's boot stomps a second time on the snow.

"But I'm scared." I hate how weak my voice sounds.

Henry wraps his arm around my shoulder. "Me too, buddy. Look at the scary world we live in. But fear has a way of nudging you toward change. And it's time, Max. Fucking bulldoze through the snow and take back what was stolen from you!"

36

Aggi

WHEN MAX SAID HE NEEDED air, I figured he had to pee, but he's been been talking to Henry for five minutes and there have been hugs and pats and kicks, and absolutely no peeing.

"Isn't that what *we're* supposed to do?" Jen asks fiddling with the heater. "Make an excuse to use a restroom, or the great outdoors, so you can talk to your friend? Fifty bucks says they're talking about us."

I smile but worry about what Max might be saying to Henry. The way Henry kicked that pile of snow has me concerned that Max regrets I'm here.

Sitting in the car with Jen settles my nerves, though. The way she points out the obvious with confidence and certainty. Maybe when I'm her age and out of my house, I'll act like that, too.

Here in the back seat listening as Jen pokes fun at the boys, the music muffled by the heater, I can't help but think of Kate.

The morning of the accident, I woke brimming with confusion. As I shuffled into the kitchen, pink fuzzy socks on my feet, I found Kate cooking breakfast for the family. She was wearing headphones and shaking her hips while she scrambled eggs. I watched her for a minute—maybe two—and smiled as she danced without a care. She caught me giggling when she turned around and rattled off: "Beyoncé made me do it!"

She didn't ask if I was hungry but pushed a plate of fluffy eggs and potato wedges topped with cheese and chives in front of me. It was my last meal at the table with my sister, but, of course, at that time, I neither knew nor appreciated it. That night, shortly after midnight, Kate would lose control of the car she was driving, spin on the ice, and drive head-on into a tree. Upon impact, Cal's chest and skull would crush.

For the next several days, I'd try to duplicate that breakfast by peeling potatoes and soaking them in water. I'd chop spuds into chunks and fry them with bacon. Sprinkle the tops with cheddar and chives and plate them with care. The breakfast was for Kate. The breakfast, a symbol of normalcy. What our life was like before chaos. But once home from the hospital, Kate would refuse to leave her room. She would stop making eye contact, too. If Kate could just take one bite of the eggs, I thought, she'd remember our time in the kitchen, when I confided in her and told her I loved Max and she insisted I tell him how I felt because he loved me, too. That morning before the accident, I had shared with Kate my plans for later that night. How Max and I were going to the science building for a picnic on the roof and how I'd bring music and candles and my big furry blanket. She laughed and said, "You're over-planning, Aggi."

Kate warned me my fantasy might not be as beautiful as I imagined. She said, "Oh, it can be great, but be realistic. It's your first time. It's going to feel a hell of a lot better for him than for you. But the second time will improve, and by the third—"

Kate was right. The first time was more painful than beau-tiful, but Max was gentle and attentive and everything you want your first to be. There's never been a second time, as death interrupted.

First, the missed messages from Kate that night:

Hey, Ag. Can you talk to Dad? He's not answering his phone. I need him to pick us up. It's beginning to snow hard.

Aggi? Did you get my message? Where are you? I need Dad to pick us up.

Did you get ahold of Dad? Is he coming?

We're not sure if we should drive. Hello?

I totally forgot you're with Max! OMG. I hate to inter-rupt, but it's sort of an emergency.

So Cal says we can make it home if we take it slow. We're going to head out now. Call me when you get this message in case we get stranded in the middle of nowhere. LOL.

Then the frantic voice mails from Dad:

Aggi? Where are you? I need you to call me back.

Aggi? There's been an accident. Mom and I are at the hospital with Kate. She's okay, but we need you here. Is Max with you?

Aggi? Dammit. Where are you? Please hurry, honey!

"Aggi?" Jen's mouth moves, but the words don't register. Her face is soft like Kate's. Her eyes full of questions. "Visiting other lands?" she asks.

I nod and wipe the tears from my eyes. "Something like that."

"I'm sorry about your sister." She glances at her folded hands, then back at my face. "Henry told me what happened."

"Thanks."

"For what it's worth, I lost my dad two years ago in May, and I'd like to say it gets easier, but that would be complete and utter bullshit." I half smile, and Jen covers my hand with hers. "I'm really glad we met," she says.

"Yeah—me too."

Cold air blasts as Henry—all smiles—climbs into the driver's seat and greets Jen with a kiss on the cheek. Max piles into the back seat, his eyes glued to the floorboard, and as he plops down, I hear "Shit." Max reaches outside the car to retrieve one of the giant shoes he's been sliding around in all night.

Five minutes on the road heading to the lake and Max leans over and whispers, "Those girls you saw at my house were not there to make you jealous."

I nod slowly. But they did. Seeing Max with someone else made me incredibly jealous. "So—what?" I say, dropping my head against the seat back.

Max matches my move. Our faces are now inches apart, but confusion and fear prevent our hearts from returning from a million-mile journey. At least that's how I feel.

"Why have you spent all these months following me?" I ask. "Is it for the lawsuit? To find shit you can use against me? Help improve your family's case? Make sure you guys win?"

Max shoots straight up in his seat.

"Win? There's no . . ." Max drops his chin. He opens his mouth, but words don't form.

"I'm sorry. I shouldn't have followed you. But for the record, it was for me, not them."

Max's eyes return to the floorboard.

"Did you ever stop to think that every time I see you, I'm reminded of what we did? If I'd only looked at my phone. One time. Checked my messages. If we hadn't been together that night." The tears dump onto my cheeks. My nose runs, and I can't bring my hand to my face to wipe anything away.

"They'd be alive," Max whispers, and scoots closer to me. He slides his hand under mine, and I grab his wrist and squeeze. Electricity shoots up my arm and wraps me in a warm afterglow of heat. "I could have looked at *my* phone, too," he says. "Cal called me, and I never checked my phone until it was too late."

Max reaches across the seat and wipes my cheeks with his thumb. I won't let go of his wrist.

"That's why I followed you around," Max says. "I knew how heavy the load was that you carried. I carried one, too. But I wanted to be there in case you needed me."

The tears flood my face. Henry glances in the rearview mirror, nods, and turns the music up so Max and I have privacy in the back seat.

I slide against the door and my head falls against the window, everything on the outside black and blurry, but when I blink, the view clears. Max unbuckles his seat belt and slides into the middle and buckles again. He drapes his arms over my back, and the weight of his body feels light compared to the burdens pushing my insides.

Kate. The guilt. The blame. My dad.

Max sweeps my hair across my neck and whispers, "It's not our fault."

If only I believed him.

Will You Think of Me?

Lyrics by Kate Frank and Cal Granger

Will you think of me and the dresses I wore?
Will you remember my laugh and how I swore?
The places we used to go
The people we used to know

Will you remember flowers in my hair?
Will you remember how much I cared?
About the food we ate
Where we met
How much we talked when we stayed up late

Will you think of me when times are tough?
Will you remember that I was once enough?
That I loved you and you loved me
Will you forget or will you think of me?

37

WE CREEP DANGEROUSLY CLOSE TO Aggi's house before turning onto a narrow stretch of road in need of a plow.

"Cut the lights," Aggi says as we pass the back side of our property and inch toward the barn.

Henry pulls the car beside one of the oversized pine trees that sit on each side of the red-and-white building. We miraculously don't get stuck thanks to the fresh set of tracks. Someone's circled the drive within the past few hours.

"Help me with the doors, man," I say as Henry and I climb out of the car. Pulling Jen's car inside the barn will lessen the risk of someone seeing us, or worse.

Henry cranes his neck, staring back over the road.

"Don't worry," I say, patting his shoulder. "We're safe here. Private property." I can't help but wonder who circled the field in front of the barn, and as I look out over the dark space, I catch Henry following the tracks with his eyes. We make eye contact, but neither mentions the mystery. We don't have to. We're both thinking the same thing. The twins have been here.

Henry pulls Jen's car inside, and Aggi retrieves a bundle of blankets from crates stacked on the side of the barn. After Henry and I latch the front doors, open the back, and start a fire in the pit, we're all feeling at ease. In fact, Henry and Jen have become so comfortable that it's making Aggi and me fidget. All their sighs and lip smacks.

Aggi's sitting on a blanket, running her hand across the wool, and I can't help but wish I were lying beside her. She catches my gaze, and we smile. Henry makes a rather disturbing sound, something like a moan, and Aggi's eyes widen.

"Want to go for a walk?" she whispers, and I jump to my feet.

We circle around the back of the barn, wandering into the dark field. Light from the fire pit flickers as we stroll, or in my case, slide—thanks to Henry's big-ass shoes—toward the trees, but once we reach the woods, the snow clears and darkness consumes us. Finally, we are completely alone.

I turn to Aggi. "I never had the chance to tell you how sorry I am about your sister. I never got to tell you . . . I tried, but . . ."

Aggi looks up at me with her big, beautiful eyes, and I feel now is the time to explain everything to her. Why I brought girls to my house though I knew she was watching me. How I thought our relationship was over and Aggi didn't care about us anymore. How I was broken on the inside and out, and the distraction of a girl at my house made me temporarily forget why I felt so broken. For a moment, I felt whole. I forgot the worry of Aggi hating me as much as her dad did. Does.

Henry's voice whirls in my head. *Fucking bulldoze through the snow.* Go after what was stolen from us. My heart wants her. My brain wants her. Every cell in my goddamn body wants Aggi, and it's time for me to bulldoze through my fears and tell her exactly how I feel.

I reach for her hand, and she lets me take it. "Aggi?"

38

Aggi

"MAX? I HAVE TO ASK you something." A thousand questions bombard my brain, but I only need the answer to one. "Do you blame me for what happened to your brother?"

Max grabs my other hand and hesitates. Standing under the trees, in complete darkness, the only sound our breathing, he whispers, "Nothing is your fault," and his words seem to echo.

"But your family blames me." A heavy weight lifts from my chest.

Max squeezes my hands. "They don't blame *you* for anything. They know we were together that night, and they know Cal and Kate tried to call us, but they don't blame us. They tried to call our dads, too."

His words, a soft blanket, wrap around my shoulders,

smothering painful memories and a year of regret. But ten seconds later, I'm cold again. "Mine do. Well, my dad blames me, us, for everything."

"I'm sorry, Aggi. I don't know what to do."

The first time Dad threatened Max, I thought he was joking, that it was the beer talking, but the next morning his words still stung. "If you care about your family, if you care about Kate, you'll never speak to him again. And if he tries to talk to you . . ."

Dad was never a violent man. A stern voice when I deserved it, but after Kate died, the tone changed. The hurt from losing his daughter shot from his mouth in the form of anger and blame.

"Your dad said he'd hurt me. His words hurt more." Max squeezes my hand again. I shiver, pull Max toward me, and he wraps me in his arms. "I'm scared, Aggi."

"It's just a threat," I whisper, although my dad's words scare me, too, sometimes. They're what's kept me from Max all these months.

"What do we do?" Max asks, and I'm unsure how to answer.

I kick at the pine straw, run my hands up and down his arms before grabbing handfuls of his coat and pulling him toward me. "I guess we'll have to figure it out together."

Max reads my cues—like clockwork—and his palm flattens against my cheek, his arm pushes at the small of my back. He pulls me into the warmth of his body, and my lips search for his. It takes only seconds for our mouths to reunite, and we kiss for the first time in a year.

Fast, frantic, breathless at first, until we find our rhythm.

His bottom lip brushes the top of mine, my tongue dancing with his.

Max tastes how I remember. Peanut butter and spearmint, soda and something bitter. He smells different, though. The smoke from the party lingering in his clothes and hair.

"Aggi," he whispers between breaths.

"Yeah," I whisper back.

"Let's." Breath. "Go." Breath. "To." Moan. "The." Breath. "Car." Breath.

"Yes. Let'sgonow!"

Holding hands, we sprint for the barn, but after a few steps, Max says, "Wait. Shit! I've lost my shoe." I pull my phone from my pocket to shine the light and notice several more messages from my dad.

"Hang on." I scan one of his messages, type back: *Be home in a while. With friends.* Although I'm angry with my dad, I don't want him to worry something's happened to me. Immediately, another message pops up from him that reads: *Home now. Not in a while.* I swipe away the bubble and shine the flashlight at the ground.

We spot Max's shoe a few feet behind us. He slips it on and grabs my hand. "Everything okay?" he asks, eyeing my phone.

I shake my head. "It won't be," I say, "but right now it's perfection."

We slip into the barn, racing for the car. Max abruptly stops and motions at the steamy windows and bare foot pressing against the glass. "Guess the car's taken," he says, and I laugh.

I stoke the fire while Max relocates the wool blanket at the side of the pit. Max's eyes connect with mine, and we smile, then quickly look away. In the dark, our desire for each other took over, but in the light of the fire, my insecurities ignite. As if reading my mind, Max sits on the blanket, arms draped over his knees, and says, "Will you sit beside me?"

I chuckle nervously and nod. As soon as I move next to him, he tilts his head, and I grab fistfuls of his coat and pull him on top of me.

Max squeals like my little sister. *Damn*, the sound is almost shocking.

39

I HAVE A BONER THE size of Florida, and if I don't stop
kissing Aggi . . .

"What? What's wrong?" Aggi asks as I break our five-
minute kiss. We're both gasping for air, and I don't want to
stop, but I'm overwhelmed with emotion. A year of separa-
tion, each day spent wondering and worrying about Aggi, if
she hates me, blames me, wishes we never were. Brokenness
was all I felt for so long. Lost without my brother, lost without
Aggi. And now here we are.

I shake my head. "Nothing's wrong." Everything's right. I
trace her lips with my finger. "It's just . . ."

Aggi's eyes are speckled with brown and green moss in
the light of the fire. Her nose is splattered with freckles that
spill onto her cheeks and will me to connect the dots with
my lips.

"Just what?" she asks, kissing me again.

"Just that you're so amazing and I can't stop looking at you. I can't stop touching your face. Everything feels like it used to, like we're back where we started yet beginning from someplace new." I shake my head. "I know. I'm not making sense."

Aggi laughs, grabbing my neck and pulling my face against hers. "I missed this face," she whispers, both hands against my cheeks. "Your eyes, your lips, your . . . everything. And I never want to be without you again."

We roll around the blanket, Aggi laughing as Henry's shoe flies from my foot and bounces off a rock lining the fire pit. Our laughter feels comfortable, as if we've never been separated. This is what they say happens when old friends reunite after months or years of distance. We start where we left off, and it's like we've never been apart.

It hits me how free I feel. Unburdened, not focused on blame. Since the accident, guilt was the only thing I'd given myself permission to feel.

Aggi climbs onto my lap, straddles Florida, and kisses my chin, cheeks, nose. "I want to stay like this forever," she whispers, and I'm so happy I nearly let out another embarrassing squeal.

Aggi slips her hand beneath my shirt and shoots it up my chest. "Those pull-ups at the library are really paying off," she says, and my smile circumnavigates my head, twice. She shifts and undoes the top button on my jeans, and I stop breathing. Seriously, no air, only a grunt.

"Are you okay?" she asks, the button paused between her fingers.

"Yeah, very okay."

"O-kay?"

"Sorry. It's just . . . I had a problem . . . or not really a problem . . . a symptom . . . no . . . never mind."

Aggi smiles. "Do you want to talk about it?"

My initial reaction is an emphatic *HELL NO!* Yet I do. I need to talk to someone about my year of brokenness, but Aggi's not that person. Next week, I'm going to tell my mom and dad that I want to see the grief counselor again, but this time by myself, so I can sit on the couch and speak freely about how I've felt, what I'm feeling, and how I'd like to feel. I want to talk openly about the brokenness I've experienced since Aggi and I had sex the first time. I want to find out if I'm okay. Tonight I feel amazing, but what about next week or the month after that? I need someone qualified to listen when I ask embarrassing-to-me questions.

"I need to say something." Aggi scoots backward on my lap and reaches for my hands. "After we—you know—had sex that night, and then . . ." I stop for a deep breath.

The best day of my life turned out to be the worst day, too. I lost my virginity and my brother the same night. While I was enjoying the best moments of my life, Cal's was ending. The incredible time Cal had told me not to push but to let happen naturally. And I would never get an opportunity to tell him about it. Every day since, all I wanted was to tell my brother how being with Aggi was everything he'd said it would be and more. "When we found out our worlds fell apart, everything broke," I say. "Including me."

Aggi nods and stares at our interlocked fingers. That's as much as I can bring myself to explain. What I thought was broken had nothing to do with Aggi, but everything to do with blame. I blamed myself, and I expected Aggi to blame me, too.

"I broke, too," she whispers, scooting closer to me again.

"I . . . Aggi . . . I . . ."

"Max . . . I . . ."

An engine purrs alongside the barn.

"Oh my God," she says, and leaps off me.

We scramble to our feet and she throws the blanket at me, and I'm not sure if she wants me to hide it or wear it like a ghost.

"What do we do?" I ask.

"Out the back?"

"And leave Henry and Jen?"

"What if it's my dad?"

Aggi's already racing toward the back door when the front ones open and in walk Umé and another girl. Jen and Henry fall out of Jen's car, and Umé shoots them a look of horror. "Great Scott Disick! What the hell is going on in here?"

"Umé!" Aggi runs toward her.

I retrieve my shoe from the fire pit and join Aggi, as I'm introduced to Umé's new college friend, Abigail. I wisecrack about the names Aggi and Abby, and nobody laughs. New girl flatly says, "Just Abigail. Never Abby."

Henry and Jen join us from the car. Jen tucks in her shirt,

and Henry buttons up his. "Missed one, champ," I say, and Henry grins, fumbling to rebutton his shirt.

After a series of awkward hellos, Aggi whispers, "We need to get out of here. Too many cars, too many voices." She's right. We're uncomfortably close to both of our homes.

"Anyone hungry?" I ask.

Someone suggests Plum Lake Café, but it's been closed for over an hour. Jen says, "I could really eat some pizza right about now," and Aggi says, "We know just the place."

The fire's dwindled to short orange flames, and I grab a shovel and toss dirt into the pit. Smoke plumes and disappears with the wind.

While we're figuring out who is riding with whom, headlights tunnel through the darkness, aiming at the barn, and Henry shouts, "Let's go!"

We scramble for the cars. Aggi and I end up with Umé and Abigail, and Henry and Jen spring back into Jen's black Honda. A tangerine Chevy pickup plows into the field, spraying slush as it heads toward us. I recognize the silhouettes— long straggly hair and bearded faces—as Henry's twin brothers. Henry shouts, "Lucio and Sons! Meet you there!"

He jams the car into drive and races for the road in front of Aggi's house.

Umé whips left to cut the twins off, and the giant tangerine circles us twice, Henry's brothers craning their necks to see who's in the car. I wave, trying to distract them, even though the last thing I'd ever want to do is have a conversation with those two assholes.

40

Aggi

WE WEAVE ON AND OFF side streets, creep down black alleys, pull into a trailer court, and park—cutting the lights—while we watch the twins whip by in their sunburst of a pickup.

"What the hell did Henry do this time?" Umé shouts from the front seat.

"They were drinking, so he took their keys." Max stares at the taillights as they disappear down the narrow country road.

"Hasn't Henry learned good intentions will get him nowhere with those two shitheads?" Umé inches from the row of mailboxes and pauses at the main road. "Wish I'd talked to Henry before texting them back. Should have known they were up to no good. He needs to stand up to them. It's the one tactic he's never tried."

"We should go back the same way we came," I interrupt. "It'll lead us to Lucio's."

"The pizza place?" Umé's friend Abigail asks.

"Best pizza in town," Umé says. "So incredible, in fact, that Aggi and I had it earlier tonight."

"Yeah," I say. "It's impossible to refuse even when you're not hungry."

Max and I watch the back window for light as Umé races toward town. The window fogs and Max and I take turns wiping it with our coat sleeves.

"They must think Henry's with us," Max says.

I shift sideways in my seat so I can eyeball what's in front and in back of us. "They don't know Jen's car, so it's perfect that Henry's not with us."

Main Street at night is dead. Store windows—those that aren't boarded up or plastered with *for rent* signs—are black, and the only open business is a lonely bar in the middle of town. As we pass that dive bar—its red, white, and blue neon sign flashing *Open*—Umé steps on the gas and yells, "Hold on!"

We shoot through a red light. Out the window, the orange truck revs its engine.

"Faster!" Max yells, and Umé cranks the wheel. I slam against the door, choked by my seat belt.

"There's a car wash at the next street!" Max shouts over the hum of the heater blasting on high.

"You want me to pull in there?" Umé yells. And I, too, question Max's idea.

234

"I don't think we should stop," I say.

Max and I know how awful Henry's brothers can be. We've watched as they've teamed up and made fun of Henry for reading books, snapping photos of the beavers on early-morning walks around the lake, and talking about strong girls with horses and swords from faraway lands. Henry's the outcast in his family—since his mother died—and frankly, the twins should see how lucky they are to have him as a brother. So he steals their keys. At least he doesn't steal for fun. Henry had his reasons for taking them. Henry always has reasons. Maybe he really didn't want the twins driving drunk. He'd seen them do it before and they'd ended up in a ditch. Henry and Max had to pull them out with Max's Jeep. Maybe Henry doesn't want their luck to run out like Cal's and Kate's did. If that isn't brotherly love, I'm unsure what it is.

Before my dad started checking my phone, Henry used to send me messages every day around the same time. I got to where I expected them, counted on them. They became a life-line. Henry and his big heart. How he wars for love but won't ever fight.

Henry never gave up on Max and me. Those messages he sent me were the only threads that held us together.

Max says he's sorry.

He hates you're going through this alone.

He wants you to know he loves you.

He'll be there, always.

My dad found Henry's text messages and warned me they were a ploy. He said Max's dad was behind those texts—trying to gather information and use it against our family—and he was convincing. He planted doubt. He told me not to communicate or he'd take away my phone for good. Dad felt threatened, but I didn't know it at the time. He put me in the middle; he wanted me to choose. Already weighted down with guilt for not answering my phone the night Cal died, I broke and succumbed to Dad's demands. Max talks about his year of brokenness, and I understand. I, too, have a year of regret.

When we finally reach Lucio's parking lot, Umé's the first brave soul to unlock and open her door. Max and I sit, waiting. He's clutching his phone and wondering why Henry hasn't called.

"Thought they stayed open late," Umé says. "After all that driving, I was totally ready for my third dinner."

41

MAX

WE'VE BEEN STANDING IN LUCIO & Sons' parking lot for thirty-five minutes with no sign of Henry and Jen or the twins, and I'm worried as shit.

"Relax," Aggi says, and I try taking a couple of deep breaths, in through the nose and out through the mouth, but knowing Henry's two brothers are looking for him makes it impossible to relax.

I grab Aggi's hand and rub her knuckles along my lips. Umé's eyebrows shoot up, and Aggi says, "Yep. We're sort of back together."

Umé snatches Aggi's arm and leads her to the other side of the car, leaving me with Umé's new friend, Abigail.

"So," I say. "You're in college?"

Abigail nods. "First year."

"Nice," I say, kicking the ground. "Fourth year. High school."

She nods, rather slowly.

My phone beeps and I tap the button, hoping it's Henry, but a message from my dad lights up the screen asking if everything's okay. I send a quick reply: All good. At Lucio's waiting for Henry.

Dad messages back: Getting late. Can you head home soon?

Then: Is Aggi with you?

I glance up as Aggi walks toward me. "Is that Henry?" Her voice sounds urgent.

I shake my head and hold up my phone. "My dad wants to know if you're with me."

"What? No. He asked you that?"

I nod, messaging my dad back. Nope.

He replies immediately: You sure?

My dad knows something. I feel it. I also feel myself getting angry at him for suddenly involving himself in my life, so I shoot another text: Why would you ask me such a ludicrous question? Since when do you check up on me?

Dad replies: Saw Dr. Nelson dropping off Grace. There's a lot of noise. Shouts coming from next door

I read the message, twice. Then: Guess I hoped Aggi was at home for her little sister's sake.

I look at Aggi, my mouth open with no words.

"What?" Aggi snaps. "What did he say?"

"He says Grace is home. He hears fighting."

Aggi digs into her pocket for her phone and swipes the screen frantically. Her eyes flutter. "Shit! Grace wanted to come home. I missed a message from Dr. N and five million from my dad. I need to get home now!"

42

Aggi

I HATE LEAVING MAX IN the parking lot—alone—but Grace can't be home without someone looking out for her. Max insisted he stay, even made it sound like it was his idea. "I need to be here when Henry and Jen show up."

The drive home drags as Abigail and Umé feel the heaviness weighing me down in the back seat. Umé pulls into the driveway and says, "Are you sure we can't come with you?"

I promise everything will be fine, and Umé insists I text later. As soon as I hit the bottom step of my porch, voices boom. Loud shouts followed by my mother's shrill cry. The front door is locked, so I dig into my pocket for my keys, but before I retrieve them, a voice calls from behind me. "Aggi? Is everything okay?" Max's dad.

The door swings open, and my dad fills the space in front of me.

"Where in the hell have you been?" he shouts, and the door across the driveway slams. I wish Mr. Granger had waited longer for an answer.

I push by Dad, scanning the living room for Grace. Mom stands by the unlit fireplace, one hand on her hip, the other bracing against the brick. "Mom?" She doesn't turn around as I pass. That's when I catch a glimpse of Grace, huddled against the wall near the table with my buds in her ears. She's hugging Cirrus to her heart while the cat squirms and tries to escape. One of Kate's old scarves wraps Grace's neck. I wave to get Grace's attention, but her eyes are glued to the back of the cat.

"Gracie!" I shout. "Let's go!"

Dad meets me toe-to-toe. "You didn't answer me," he says. "Where have you been all night? I've been trying to reach you."

"With friends," I mumble, grabbing Grace's arm and pulling her toward me. She plants herself on the hardwood, drawing lines in the dust with her feet as I desperately urge her to stand.

"Your phone is worthless if you're not going to answer it."

Dad's harsh words pierce my heart. This is where the fights always end up: blaming me for not picking up the phone the night of the accident. News flash, Dad. You didn't pick up either.

Grace jerks her arm from me and scoots under the table. "Grace," I say, "we're staying at Dr. Nelson's tonight."

Dad stomps forward. "You're not going anywhere! Grace

wanted to come home, and we want her here with us."

The anger bubbles inside me. Why? To fight in front of her? Avoid giving her the attention she needs? Become the perfect little stick family we believed we once were?

I point an accusatory finger at my father. "All you do is fight." My voice echoes. "I heard you in the driveway! Why would you do that in front of Grace? She's under the table wearing earbuds."

My father mumbles, and I smell tonight's beer on his breath. His eyes are red, but I can't tell if it's alcohol induced or if he's been crying. Probably both.

"Dad." I try to steady my voice and keep it calm. "Please stop fighting in front of her. She's hardly ever at home anymore. Why would you waste precious time?"

Dad shakes his head like he's trying to remove the words I've spoken from his memory. He orders me to my room.

"No!" I shout, pushing past him. He grabs my elbow, and the tight grip on my funny bone jolts my arm with pain. "Stop it!" I shout, tears spilling down my cheeks. "Just stop! Dad, please!"

"Let her go!" a voice rings out, high-pitched and full of rage. "Let her go now!" I expect to see my mother but instead see Grace charging us. She pounds her fists into Dad's back. He turns, wobbling from the beer, and before I can dive in front of him to protect my sister, his arm flies up and accidentally knocks Grace onto the floor. At least I hope it was accidental. Grace lands on her bottom with eyes the size of saucers, teeth shivering in fear.

"See what you made me do?" Dad shouts, spittle hitting my face.

"Made who?" Mom steps forward, and for a minute I think maybe she's going to scoop Grace into her arms and protect us from who my father has become since Kate died, but she starts yelling about what's wrong with him, how he's turned into someone unrecognizable.

I run over to Grace and wrap my arms around her. "Are you okay?" I whisper, crawling beneath the table. She rocks quietly, hugging her knees, and I promise her things will get better. As I'm whispering to Grace, I realize I'm promising myself, too.

More shouts. Fingers pointed, cocked with guilt.

My head pounds with chaos, but I shield my hands over Grace's earbuds and hold my sister as tight as she'll allow.

Before long, Dad's back in my face slinging accusations. "You were with *him*! That's why you didn't call me back. Just like you were with him the night his brother died. If you hadn't been with him . . ."

I refuse to scream; I can do that later in the woods.

I refuse to run; Grace needs her big sister.

I refuse to cry, but my tears ignore my pleading.

"It wasn't our fault," I murmur under my breath. "It wasn't anybody's fault."

I stare blankly at my father, and as he continues to rant, I block his words with mine. "You're wrong," I say. "It was an accident." When I look at Dad's face, the lines running parallel on his forehead, etches spilling from the corners of his mouth and plummeting toward his chin, the truth surfaces. It's been visible for months, but tonight it's under a spotlight. Dad, afraid of what will happen if Max and I find each other again. Dad, afraid of losing control like Kate lost control of the car that spun on the ice. He believes he won't lose me if I'm under his restraint, but the more he tries, the more unreasonable, uncontrollable he becomes.

I crawl out from beneath the table and call to him calmly. "Dad." I don't know how to continue or even if I should, but I have to explain that what he's doing is destroying his family. "Dad."

He turns toward me as a fist pounds on the front door. "Aggi! Mr. Frank! Open up!"

Max.

43

HENRY INSISTED THIS WAS a bad idea, and I reminded him that we spent the better half of the night running from the choice he made to take the truck keys belonging to his brothers. Henry's response: "Well, I did lose my virginity tonight, so there's that." I'm afraid Henry's going to be using that line for the remainder of the year.

"Max," Henry says as we're climbing out of Jen's car. "Your dad and your mom are on the front porch."

I glance over at my house. "Max!" my dad shouts, and I ignore him like he's ignored this situation for too long.

I march up Aggi's front steps, Henry following behind me. Mr. Frank's voice blasts as I raise my fist and hover it over the door.

"You sure?" Henry asks.

"Max!" my dad shouts. If he wants to stop me, he's going to have to confront his own fears.

I nod at Henry, my heart revving in my chest, and pound on the door, shouting, "Aggi! Mr. Frank! Open up!"

By my sixth knock, the door swings open and Mr. Frank's bloodshot eyes pierce mine. Across the driveway, my dad shouts my name again, but I force myself to hold Mr. Frank's gaze.

Words I should have spoken a year ago fly from my mouth. "I came to see if Aggi's okay."

Mr. Frank's glazed eyes. My father's shouts. Henry, breathing hard from the steps. Grace's whimpers from somewhere inside the house. An engine growing louder on the lake road. My dad, again. Cal, Kate, Aggi.

My hands squeeze into fists.

"I am here to see Aggi!"

44

Aggi

WHEN GRACE HEARS MAX'S VOICE, she jumps to her feet and Cirrus leaps from her arms, zigzagging across the living room floor, scrambling for the door. Grace shouts for Cirrus, and Mom squats to block the cat from darting outside.

Dad turns, witnessing the commotion, and I catch a glimpse of Max at the door. "What the hell is he doing here?" Dad asks me, pointing accusingly.

"I told you why I was here," Max answers.

Cirrus cries and hisses. Mom lets the cat go, and Cirrus zips between Dad's legs.

"Goddamn cat!" Dad shouts, kicking Cirrus onto the porch.

Grace screams and rushes for the cat, but Cirrus leaps from the steps and disappears into the darkness.

Dad yells, "You get off my property or I'm calling the police," but Max won't back down.

"I'm not going anywhere, sir. . . . I need to see if Aggi's okay."

"Nobody's okay," I snap as I stare at my dad. He's surprisingly calm now, so I continue. "I was at a party tonight on the lake. Grace fell into the water—or maybe she jumped—I don't know, but Max dived in and saved her." My dad shoulders the wall, and I inch toward Max. "If Max hadn't been there . . ." I hesitate, watching my dad's face contort. All the lines I saw earlier now blending together. His eyes water.

"Get out of my house!" he shouts, and his shoulders and body slump, as if the words have drained his energy.

For a second, I'm unsure whom Dad is ordering out of the house, and when I look at Max, he nudges toward the door with his head. The urge to run swallows me.

I glance back at the living room, searching for Grace. Mom sits stiff on the couch, hands clutched in her lap, mumbling how sorry she is. Mom—similar to Dad—only has energy enough to focus on one daughter at a time: the one she lost.

How I miss my mother. Her hugs. The scent of her flowery perfume rubbing against my face, lingering long after I fall asleep. I walk to her and kneel, whispering, "I know you're sorry, but you don't need to be. We just need *you*. I need you. Grace needs you." Her eyes unlock from her hands, and I clutch her bony fingers. "I love you, Mom."

Dad's crying hard now. A hand spread across his face. I call Grace's name, but there's no answer.

"Let's go, Gracie! Get your coat! Time to head back to Dr. Nelson's!" I have no intention of driving to Dr. Nelson's house at this hour of the night. I plan to drive around the lake until Grace falls asleep in the car. Then I'll text Umé and see if she'd mind houseguests for the night. But I need to find Grace so we can leave this house.

As I pass the front door, the orange Chevy flares in the drive and the twins spill out, flanking Henry. He towers above them. "Max?" I say, and signal with my thumb.

Then I scan the room again for Grace and race up the stairs, leaving my dad slumped against the wall, holding his head in his hands. I won't let him stop me this time. I should have done this months ago.

When I reach Grace's bedroom, the door's shut and locked. "Grace?" I call, knocking on the door. "Open up. Time to go."

Nothing.

"Come on, Grace! Get your coat! We're leaving!"

Silence, followed by Dad's boots on the stairs.

"Aggi!"

I draw a deep breath, turn, and face Dad leaning against the railing at the top of the stairs. "I'm taking Grace back to Dr. Nelson's. We're both going to stay there awhile. You and Mom need time alone. Time to sort things out." My voice is steady, even, the truth stuffed inside me. I want to beg him to go back to counseling and get the help he needs processing

249

the suffering he feels. My parents can't do it alone. My dad has alienated himself, and my mother, from everyone who might help ease their pain. But Grace and I can't stay here and hope they'll one day improve. I've lived their limitations for a year. Tonight, I'm leaving, but not without my little sister.

"You're not going anywhere," Dad says, walking down the hallway toward me. "His family wants to hurt us. They keep hurting us. Don't you see that?"

Dad's dangerously close but his voice surprisingly flat.

Feeling encouraged, not by his words but that he's speaking instead of yelling, I reply, "Max has nothing to do with your war against his dad."

Dad winces and I recoil. "Max is part of *that* family!" Dad shouts, and the way he spits "that" sounds like a hard-hitting expletive.

"Remember at the hospital, Dad? You told Kate it wasn't her fault. You said Cal didn't die because of her. And Kate didn't die because of Max, his family, or anyone else!"

Dad groans, spins around, and smacks the wall. As he turns, I see Max at the bottom of the stairs. Dad sees him, too. Then my mother joins.

Dad stares at their faces, then back at mine. He shouts, "I miss her! I want her back!" and raises his fist. Max misreads Dad's clenched hand and charges the stairs, as my father punches the wall next to me, his fist digging deep into plaster, spraying dust into my face.

"James!" my mother shouts.

The impact stuns Dad, and he falls onto his knees, shaking, crying. Max grabs me. "Are you okay?" I nod, but I'm unsure I am.

Max says, "Where's Grace?"

I kick at the bottom of Grace's door, shouting her name, but she won't answer.

Max jumps up and wiggles the handle, pounds on the door. "Grace! Baby girl! We need you to open up!"

My mother stares at my dad balled up on the floor. Her face is sunken, eyes gray. She hasn't slept a full night since the accident, but it's only now that I see how frail she's gotten these past few months. Instead of crumpling to the floor like my father, my mother tightens her lips, and her chest expands as she draws a breath and turns her head toward me. For a second, we connect. Her eyes fixate on my face, then move quickly to Grace's door as she marches to Grace's bedroom, kicking the box of nails that explodes on impact. She slams her body against the wood.

"We need something to open the door with," I say as Mom slams her shoulder and hip against the door.

Mom shouts, "There's a crowbar in the kitchen!"

Max flies down the stairs as Mom steps back and kicks Grace's door handle, trying to break it from the wood.

Dad, huddled against the wall, glances up at us, lifeless, the color drained from his face. "Maybe she's not there," he whispers, and I'm certain it's his way of offering words to comfort me, Mom, himself.

251

Dad's the one who found Kate that horrible morning in her room. It took three minutes for him to bust down the door. Three minutes that will haunt him the rest of his life. One hundred and eighty seconds. Were they the difference between life and death? If Dad had shown up earlier, would Kate still be alive? We've all given much thought to those three minutes, but we've never talked about them since they passed.

Grace and I were only a few seconds behind Dad when he stormed Kate's door. Mom blocked the doorway, preventing us from going in, when Dad shouted on repeat, "Oh my God, no, oh my God, no!" All color from Mom's face drained, and I knew it was bad, but didn't know how much until I heard Kate's body spill onto the floor. The thud plays like a drum in my head, like Dad's repeated words of shock. *Thud. Thud. Thud.* When I'm in bed. *Thud. Thud. Thud.* When I'm walking in the woods. *Thud. Thud. Thud.* When I'm trying to study. I never want to hear that sound again, or the screams that followed.

Max flies up the stairs with the crowbar. My mother shouts, "Here!" and yanks the tool from his hands. She wedges the metal shaft into the door, and within seconds, it pops open. "Oh, God!" Mom yells, and my dad scrambles to his feet.

I peek into Grace's empty room. Her window is propped open, the cold air rippling her blinds. Dad races for the window, pops his head out, and stares into darkness. The only light beams from Max's front porch.

"Grace!" Dad shouts out the window, and Mom orders us downstairs.

We race toward the front door. On the porch, Henry stands at the railing while his twin brothers sit on the top step like they've been ordered not to move.

Max shouts, "I have to get a pair of boots," and Henry shoots off the porch, yelling, "I'm on it!"

I walk between the twins and check the rockers, expecting Grace to be sitting in one of them, but no such luck.

Dad says, "Here," and hands me a flashlight, then turns to my mother. "Emmy, call me if Grace shows up."

Mom, slipping into her coat, snaps, "I'm going with you to find my baby and bring her back home where she belongs."

Dad's right, though: we need someone at home in case Grace returns. Max reads my mind and says, "My mom. I'll get my mom. She'll come over and wait for Grace."

I expect my father to shout, "Over my dead body," but Dad nods and waves us into the driveway, saying, "We'll find her. She's going to be okay."

Dad's words slam into me like a wall of snow. Why wouldn't Grace be okay? The lake, Grace falling, or maybe jumping, into the water, how she screamed when Dad grabbed my elbow and later kicked Cirrus. I wrap my arms around my head. Even the finest threads holding my family together now fray and unravel. Max steps beside me. "She's going to be fine. She just didn't want to hear them fight anymore."

Dad stomps to the back of the house, and Max and I follow.

Henry jogs across the driveway with a pair of Max's boots. Once they're on, Max jogs into the field heading toward the barn.

The snow sprays a light dusting, and the moon plays hide-and-seek behind gray-and-black clouds. We're all shouting Grace's name. My mom, Dad, Henry, Max, and even the twins. We circle the house and split up in the driveway.

I zigzag through the pine trees standing like giants near the mailbox. Their branches wide and trunks straight as spines. When we were little, Max and I pretended they were guardians of the forest. Giants sent from distant lands to protect our families from whatever imaginary creature lived in the woods. I wonder if Grace thinks about the trees as her protectors. I wonder what she thought before she ended up in the lake.

"Grace!" I shout, but my voice sinks into the snow like a brick.

"Grace!" Dad shouts from across the driveway, his voice causing the floodlights on Max's garage to switch on.

Shining my flashlight across the light blanket of snow in search of footprints, I shout Grace's name again and march to the edge of the driveway. I hear barks, and when I turn, Max's dad is lingering on his front steps as Pawtrick Swayze rushes toward me with his tail swinging and belly dragging the snow.

At the back of the house, the dog catches me, and I pat his head before making a beeline to Grace's window. Faint footprints circle in the snow before jetting out toward the field in front of our house. My stomach sinks. "She's at the lake!" I shout. *Oh, God. Grace is at the lake.*

I take off running, with Pawtrick Swayze on my heels. My family, Max's parents, race toward me. We meet in the driveway and I shout again, "She's at the lake!"

Max's dad asks, "What happened?"

I answer: "Grace ran away. I think she's at the lake."

My dad, the last to arrive in the driveway, snaps, "Where on the lake?"

Max's dad reaches down to snatch Pawtrick Swayze's harness and scoop his barreled body into his arms. He whispers, "The blue dock, Aggi." His words are rushed as he circles around me—distancing himself from my father—and as he passes by me, he says, "Max has seen Grace near the blue dock where the beavers used to nest. The one your dad used to take you to." Mr. Granger speed-walks toward his front porch.

We quit visiting the blue dock where the beavers lived. Dad was busy building a business with Max's father, and I was busy wanting to be alone with Max. Kate and Cal were always practicing their music, and nobody had time to spend sitting and watching the beavers. But that didn't stop Grace from begging. "When can we go back to the blue dock, Dad? I want to see the *little people*," she'd plead. Dad's grandfather used to call the beavers that roamed Plum Lake "the little people." Back then the beavers outnumbered the families living around the lake. They made their homes permanent

255

and lived generation after generation. They never moved away like people did, just built strong family structures and defended their territory.

I should have known Grace would visit the beavers by herself. She knew the trail better than I did.

Before the accident, the three of us—Kate, Grace, and I—sat on lawn chairs in the front yard feasting on s'mores while Dad hammered away on Sheetrock in the living room or upstairs. I can't remember now which room Dad was working on at the time, but Grace started in about the beavers. How *Daddy* was just like the daddy beaver. Kate would humor Grace and probe while I'd suck the sticky marshmallow paste off my fingers. "Oh, yeah, Gracie. How's that?" Grace would explain how the daddy beaver builds his house—sticks and mud—not going too deep with details, but to her it was a powerful structure. "He'll spend all day, probably the nighttime, too, making it strong and perfect for his family."

Thinking about this now, how our home is literally crumbling from the inside out, walls with holes, floorboards that scream for nails, I wonder what went through Grace's mind when Mom and Dad—though especially Dad—stopped working on the house. How that same box of nails sat in the hallway collecting powdery dust until tonight, when Mom kicked the hell out of it.

Everything stopped when Kate died. As a family, we stopped, but Grace kept moving, shuffling back and forth between Dr. Nelson's and a house that was falling apart.

A few weeks ago, Grace came home for the night and I was sitting in the bathroom, reading, while she took a bath. She said, "Dad doesn't remodel the house anymore, does he?"

I shook my head and said, "He's got a lot on his mind."

"More important things?" Grace asked knowingly.

"Yeah. More important things."

Grace paused for a moment, considered my words, then slid beneath the water, bubbles popping above her face.

Oh, Grace. Please hang on until we find you.

45

Aggi

AT THE BLUE DOCK, THE water shines like obsidian rock under the moonlight. Chunks of ice float in the deeper pockets of the lake. The headlights on Dad's truck reflect off the water and shine across the spotty snow-covered bank. "No footprints," I say. "I don't think she's been here."

Dad scans the dock and his eyes land on the lake. I look at Mom, neither of us wanting to give place to the thoughts inside Dad's head.

But the way Grace looked at me tonight after we pulled her out of the lake makes me unsettled. Grace, floating in the cold water like a doll tossed into the lake by a child wanting to see how long it would take to sink. I shudder.

"Dad. We need to check the dock at Connor's."

The drive is agonizing. It's only a few minutes away, but my mind drags me into the dark places where time stands still.

Kate used to tease Grace about the color of snow. "What color are snowflakes, Grace?" Kate would ask. "What color is the snow?" Grace would scoop a ball into her hand and gaze at it like it was something magical.

"White?" Grace knew the answer wasn't so obvious, but in the daylight when all you see is a blanket of powder and the ball you're holding looks as though it's made of sugar, what else would a five-year-old say? "Yeah, white."

"Are you sure?" Kate would question in a funny, high-pitched voice that always made me giggle. "Final answer?" She'd ruffle Grace's hair and wink in my direction. Kate had a way of bringing us together. Three sisters, years apart, yet closer than the water molecules that form an ice crystal.

Grace squeezed a chunk of snow in her tight little fist, watched as the whiteness melted and turned to water. "No!" she'd protest. "Snow has no color. It's clear!"

Kate would tuck her hands under Grace's armpits and lift her toward the sky. "You're a genius, Gracie. Snow is transparent! And you're the smartest five-year-old I know."

Grace is transparent.

She's never hidden what she felt. She's a child. Afraid. Alone. Desperately searching for order in the chaos.

When we reach the dock at Connor's, it's empty and there's no sign of Grace.

"This is where she fell?" Dad asks, and I ignore the worry in his voice.

Max's dad was sure Grace would be at the blue dock. Where the beavers used to nest. Where Dad used to take us. Maybe we didn't look hard enouth.

"We should go back," I say. "I know where she is."

46

I'M STILL SEARCHING THE BARN and the nearby field when I hear the engine of Mr. Frank's truck rev. "Henry!" I shout. "Tell them to wait!"

I need to go with Aggi. I need to help her find Grace.

I race through the field as Henry rounds the corner of my house, shouting, "She's at the lake!"

"We need the boat," I say, and spin around. I can't think straight, but I don't have time not to.

My front door opens, and my mom storms down the steps in her boots and coat. She shouts at my father as she stomps into the driveway. "You're just going to sit there? That's not the man I married. That's not the man I know."

As she passes Henry and me, my dog cuts in front of her, chasing Aggi's cat. "Pawtrick!" I shout, and he stops, drops onto his haunches.

"One of you help me get Cirrus into the house. I'll be next door in case Grace returns," Mom says. Henry waits for me to move, and I wait for him. Seeing my mom marching to Aggi's like nothing ever happened, like there isn't a tumultuous history that's haunted us for a year, freezes me. "Well, don't just stand there like your father!" she shouts. "Grab that cat, hitch up the boat, and move your asses!"

Mom's orders shoot us across the yard. Henry shouts at the twins and they come running. He scoops up Cirrus and hands the cat to one of his brothers, then orders him to take the animal to Aggi's house. I back my Jeep up to the boat and trailer and jump out, ready to hitch.

"Let me do that." I turn as Dad zips his coat.

47

MAX

DAD HITCHES THE BOAT, AND I drive while Henry calls Connor and Umé and demands the twins follow us to the dock. We need all the horsepower and search power we can get. I refuse to allow myself to stop and think about what could happen, only what I hope will. We *will* find Grace. She *will* be okay. Alternate endings are too much for any of us to bear.

In minutes, we reach the lake. The blue dock is colorless until the headlights unveil a sleek shine. But nobody's here. The only sound, the splashing water against the wood.

"Where are they?" Henry asks. Windows down, we scan the darkness and the lake.

"Connor's dock," I say, putting the Jeep into reverse and stepping on the gas.

We back away from the dock as lights zip across the lake coming toward us.

"Wait!" my dad shouts, and we jump from the Jeep.

Connor and another guy tear in on Jet Skis, cutting their engines as they pull alongside the dock. Everyone shouts at once until I yell, "Shut up! We have to find Aggi!"

Connor points and all heads turn.

Aggi and her parents pull in and jump out of the truck. Aggi shouts, "Everyone in the boat! I know where she is!"

All adults move into action, including our fathers. They don't speak to each other, but they don't fight, either.

Aggi grabs the wet suits we've stored in the boat for years. She races toward the back of her dad's truck, ripping her shirt off before reaching the cab. I look away but only to strip off my shirt and pants in the middle of the dock, then realize there's no wet suit at my feet.

Aggi stomps back toward the boat, her wet suit squeaking as she walks. She tosses her clothes into the boat and motions me over. "Come on!" Still in my underwear, I clutch my jewels and leap into the boat as Aggi throws the wet suit at my chest and we pull away from the dock.

48

Aggi

MAX INSISTS GRACE IS NOT in the water. "I've seen her where the beavers used to nest," he says. His words are unable to provide the comfort I need, though they confirm what his dad said. My mother's face, my dad's eyes—in the lights from the boat and moon—illuminate with worry.

Max reaches for my hand as if he knows what I'm thinking. He has the same thoughts but speaks only positive words.

When we reach the brushy lakeshore, Max and I are the first to jump into the water.

Dad shines floodlights, Max's father anchors the boat and grabs two flashlights, and my mother jumps in behind us. We scramble for the shore as Connor helps beam light from his Jet Ski.

As we hike along a matted trail, spotty with snow, Max and

I wind around the lakeshore, sidestepping up a slick slope. Henry slides, shouting, "Shit! My shoes won't make it!"

As we move in a line, me and Max in the lead—everyone shouting Grace's name—the sticks and grass grow thicker.

"Grace! It's Aggi!"

A rock spashes in the water.

49

Aggi

WE HUDDLE BENEATH THE DAM. Quiet, still, as we shine a light on a mud-stained tennis shoe poking out just below the nesting chamber. Max whispers, "The first time I saw Grace out here, I thought she was one of the damn beavers. Then I saw her hair and the stick in her hand she used to prod at the bank. I shouted her name and she scrambled deeper into the sticks. I climbed up to the top to check on her and she told me she wanted to be left alone. I asked her what she was doing here all by herself, and she said, "'Making sure my family has food.'"

Max wades through the weeds and suddenly disappears beneath the water.

"Max!"

He springs up out of the lake, choking and reaching for a

branch. "There's a drop here. Comes up real fast. Be careful."

I dog-paddle toward Max, around a tree that's uprooted, sprigs sticking out of the water. We break away from our parents, Henry, and the twins. Max shouts, "You guys crawl up the bank. It's unsafe for you to be in the water without a wet suit."

"Grace!" I shout, and we hear a shuffle; then another rock splashes into the water.

I shine the light up the bank and glimpse the rolled cuffs on the bottoms of Grace's pants. Her feet moving upward, disappearing into the dam. "Up there," I say, pointing up the slope.

Max pushes farther away from the shore, floating backward and circling the dam. I steady my flashlight on the hill, making the spot visible as Max crawls on top of the mountain of sticks.

"Leave me alone!" Grace shouts.

"Gracie," Max calls. "You can't stay in a beaver den."

"This is my home! Go away!" Her feet scramble.

I move from the bank and wade out toward the dam, sticks and debris sloshing as I climb to the spot where Max and Grace sit. Grace's back smashes against the wall in the deepest part of the den—where beavers go to nest—and her heels dig into the dirt to hold her there. On my hands and knees, I ease beside Max, squatting above the waterline. His hands grapple for Grace's feet as she slides forward, but she kicks at his fingers and shoves herself deeper into the den, away from Max and the light. The ground, packed with mud, is dry in spots, and in the corner of the den sit jars of peanut butter and marshmallow cream. Two large bags of yeast rolls wait to be spread. Grace's den is neatly organized—like her bedroom—with all the ingredients needed to make fluffer-nutter sandwiches. Along one wall of the den sit two six-packs of bottled water and three rolls of toilet paper. Grace has made a home for herself. A place she plans to stay. She's found a new, improved family. One that won't fight in front of her or shove her away.

"Wow, Grace." I shine the light into the chamber. "This is the coolest place I've ever seen."

A grunt.

"You've outdone yourself."

Another grunt.

"But it's cold and you don't have fur. You can't live outside. This place belongs to the beavers."

"And I belong with them!" Grace shouts.

Max inches closer. "But Grace." His voice is tender and soft. The only tone he's ever used when speaking to my little sister. "You know the beavers won't come back to their den if you're in here. They'll move. Build another den somewhere else. Maybe on the other side of the lake."

Grace is silent.

My shoes slip when I crawl toward her. "Don't try it, Aggi," Grace snaps. "You won't fit."

I lean against the bank, my shoulder pressing into the

packed mud and sticks. "Max and I don't want to make you leave, Grace. Not if you don't want to. You just come out when you're ready." Max tilts his head toward me, and I shrug. I don't know how to convince Grace that she should leave. What is there to come back home to? Grace hasn't had a home since Mom sent her to live with Dr. Nelson. She's been betrayed by both her parents. After Dad accidentally shoved her, Grace might never want to leave this den. "Maybe we could have a fluffernutter sandwich before we go? Maybe I could make one for you like I used to?"

Max squeezes my shoulder, and we wait for Grace's next move.

It's only seconds before Grace emerges from the den, saying, "Well, I am starving."

We huddle at the opening of the beaver den, the three of us, with fingers covered in sticky marshmallow cream. The cold prevents the cream from spreading, so our sandwiches consist of one large ball of marshmallow goo plopped on top of the bread like a planet surrounded by a galaxy of peanut butter.

"Too bad we can't heat up these sandwiches," Max says.

Grace holds up a cream-smothered hand in Max's face. "We can't light a fire here," she says in an accusatory voice. "This place would shoot up in flames!"

Slowly Grace inches out of the nesting chamber, her teeth chattering as she scoots between us. Her upper lip is white from the cold marshmallow paste, and when she talks, tiny threads of cream stick between her lips. "These are delicious," she says with a smack.

"Not as delicious as the ones Kate made," I say. "Remember those?"

"Do I?" Grace's voice pitches with excitement. "They were at least an inch thick. All bubbly and warm."

"And the way she toasted them on the griddle. Oh my God, Max. Did you ever eat one of Kate's grilled fluffernutters?"

Max shakes his head, nose aimed at the ground as he wipes his eyes. "I remember Cal saying they were the best sandwiches he'd ever had." Max runs his knuckle across his cheek. "And if they're as good as these . . . ," he says, holding the ball of bread and hard marshmallow into the air.

Voices carry in the distance. Our parents, getting close.

A Jet Ski engine whirrs, and Grace scrambles back to the top of the den. More voices as Max crawls down the bank, waving his arms and shouting, "We have her! She's over here!"

"I can't go back, Aggi," Grace cries. "Please don't make me go."

I flip onto my stomach and slide into the narrow slice of the den. The fit is tight, and Grace is squished into the darkest corner. I reach for her ankles to hold myself in place, but Grace mistakes my grappling for a sneak attack.

"Aggi, please!" she yells. "Don't make me go with Dad! I'm scared of him!"

Grace aged a decade this year, or so it seemed, but seeing her crouched in the den, knees tucked to her chest, trying to shrink so Dad won't see her, I remember she's my little sister and only ten. Dad scared us all after Kate died, but his evolution made the strongest impact on Grace. She watched as our house fell apart, Mom pushed her away, and Dad became a monster. If anyone deserves to be in this den alone, it is my father. He owes everyone an apology, but most of all Grace. I wonder if Dad's capable of rebuilding the family he broke.

"She's up here!" I hear Max shout, followed by splashes. My dad is the first to reach the den, his voice hoarse from crying as he shouts my sister's name. Max's dad slides his arm around his son, and I watch as they hug and follow my father to the edge of the den.

"I'll take care of you," I whisper to Grace. "I'll make sure Dad never hurts any of us again."

50

MAX

AGGI'S DAD CLUTCHES GRACE IN his arms and mumbles words like "sorry," "forgive," "love," and "precious." He sniffs and chokes on his own snot and apologies. It angers me to see him with Grace. She's a kid. Kids forgive. Doesn't mean they should. He's talking to Grace about how he's messed everything up, how he's sorry and wants to make it better somehow. He offers promises but no solutions. Grace is shaking her head like she won't believe him. She demands the same solutions we all need. Tangible results that will make her feel wanted, secure, and loved.

It took coaxing to get Grace out of the den, but Aggi crawled inside the covering and called for me, and the three of us huddled like a goddamn family of beavers. I told Gracie she was like a sister to me, and she climbed onto my lap and squeezed my neck. I told her I needed a sister. "I lost my brother, Gracie. And you lost Kate. Maybe we can be brother and sister now?" Grace grabbed my face with her sticky marshmallow fingers and squished my cheeks, her big eyes searching mine until they locked onto something familiar, something she could trust.

"Promise me we'll stick together," she said. "You and Aggi, too."

I promised. Never will I split from the person I love because of someone else's anger. Aggi's dad hasn't spoken to me, and I'm taking his silence as an unspoken agreement that he has no say in my life or in Aggi's. But an apology would feel better.

Henry meets me at the back of the twins' truck as everyone stands around waiting for Grace and her father to climb down from the den. His brothers walk by and pat Henry's shoulder.

"What the hell happened?" I ask Henry, eyeballing the twins as they climb into the cab of the pickup.

Henry shrugs and kicks the ground. "Guess I took my own advice. Told them they deserved better. We all do. Just because my grandpa taught my dad to settle his scores by punching people didn't mean they had to. I said, 'Look at Max and Cal. They were best friends.' I told them I wanted brothers like that." Henry clears his throat. "They laughed at me, as they do, but they listened when I said, 'If I really wanted to, you know I could kick your asses blindfolded and hog-tied. . . .'"

Dad walks over and wraps his arm around me. "Excuse

me, Henry—I'd like to talk to Max for a minute."

As soon as I turn toward Dad, he says, "I'm sorry."

We pause and I nod. "It's okay."

"You're amazing, Maxwell. Always quick to forgive." He glances at his feet, kicks his toe in the sticks. "We're going to get through this, Max. I promise. Things will be different."

"How, Dad?" I need more than a promise. Promises break. They shatter, and the pieces are impossible to find.

Dad lifts my chin. "I'm not exactly sure how. But I'm going to figure it out. Me and your mom." Dad draws me close, and I hug him back. His arms have been lifeless for months, too weak to lift or wrap around me, but when he squeezes my back, he feels like the strongest man I've ever known.

A throat clears, and my dad looks up and slides his hands off my back. Mr. Frank nods as Aggi walks beside me and snakes her arm around my waist. She stares at her dad, and he won't drop her gaze. I hold my breath, unsure if I should jump away from Aggi and dart behind Dad or stand with my feet planted, unwilling to move. A part of me has already dived into the lake again, but this time to get away from the towering tree in front of me. Mr. Frank swallows and glances at the ground. When he looks up again, he nods, and I know it's safe to wrap my arms around Aggi. I've wanted to hug her since we left the barn. Tell her how much I've missed her, how much I love her.

The emotions grow too intense, and I'm not sure how to process any of them. Minutes ago I was in a beaver den eating a fluffernutter sandwich with Aggi and telling Grace I'd look out for her like a big brother. Earlier, I was in the barn with Aggi, aching to love her. And at the beginning and end of this night, I jumped into a lake out of fear and love. My chest constricts, and I bend over, hands on my knees. I'm going to pass out. Aggi steps back, and my dad wraps his arm around me.

"I need to get him home," Dad says, and Mr. Frank suddenly jumps into action.

"To the boat!" Mr. Frank shouts, picking up Grace and setting her on one of the seats. He grabs a life vest and snaps it around her chest. Aggi's mom holds out a hand and helps me into the boat.

Aggi climbs on board, and I try to scoot over so she can sit next to me, but I'm lifeless on the bench. The only strength I have holds my head halfway up, and as soon as the boat pulls away from the dock, I slump onto my side and stare blankly at the black sky until we reach the other side of the lake.

Cal. Kate. Grace. Aggi.

Two gone. Two nearly lost from my life forever.

"Hey," Aggi whispers, kneeling beside me. "You okay?"

I make a noise, but I'd hardly call it a word. Aggi twists a strand of hair around her hand, leans forward, and says, "You're always there. Even when you're not supposed to be."

I smile, and she brushes my bangs.

"This hell we've been going through isn't just going to make us stronger. It's going to make us better."

I reach for Aggi's hand, and my arm flops to my side out of sheer exhaustion. Maybe she's right, but now I have no strength left in my body.

"Easy," she whispers into my ear, and every cell in my body ignites.

When we pull up alongside the dock, Dr. Nelson and my mom walk toward us from the house. My mom must have called her. Aggi's dad ties up the boat with the help of my father. The two don't speak, but their teamwork does. Grace heads for the dock, high-fiving me on the way. Aggi's mom and Dr. Nelson hug, as she thanks her for coming. They both turn to embrace Grace, and she hesitates, uncertain whom to run to first.

Dr. Nelson folds her hands and takes a step back, and Aggi's mom shouts, "Gracie girl! Come here, honey!" That's all Grace needs to hear to dive into her mother's arms.

"Let me help you, son," Mr. Frank says, extending a hand. Aggi swats it away and says, "He's fine, Dad." Then she reaches out and pulls me to my feet.

"Max." Aggi's dad. A slight scowl, but his eyes are soft.

Aggi cuts in front of me. "Dad." A full scowl and piercing eyes.

Mr. Frank nods. My dad glances in our direction.

"Thank you, Maxwell. Aggi said you rescued Grace from the lake tonight. Twice now, I think."

I slow-nod. No words. *You're welcome* doesn't seem fitting.

"I've messed up," Mr. Frank says, and I'm unsure if he's still talking to me or to Aggi. "I hurt your dad, your mom, you. I made a lot of choices that didn't help anyone. Not sure if any of you will ever forgive me."

Both our moms are watching, and my dad turns to them

and smiles. So many sad eyes, tearstained cheeks. Everyone worn from a year of heartache. To survive even one more day, we're going to need help. Every single one of us.

I look at Mr. Frank's face, his eyes watery with grief and something else, something deeper than I can comprehend. I've listened to his anger for a year. I've sat on my front porch and heard his shouts at his wife, at Aggi, at Grace. Why did he get to unleash his feelings while I kept mine stuffed somewhere inside me? So many times I wanted to storm his porch, pound my fist on the door, and shout at him to stop. So many times I made it to the driveway, then recoiled in fear.

I step forward and squeeze my fingers into fists. "I don't know about the rest of us, but I'm not sure if I *can* forgive you. At least not right now." My dad approaches, and I hold my palm up. He stops.

Mr. Frank nods, and I continue. "You hurt Aggi, Grace, both our families. Why? You were like a dad to me. I looked up to you." My whole body trembles. "We all lost someone we loved, but you managed to make the loss even worse."

Aggi moves beside me but not to interrupt. She demands answers, too. And when she shakes her head, her eyes full of disappointment, Mr. Frank wipes his eyes and says, "I've been a real asshole, and I'm sorry."

51

Aggi

Six weeks later

WE MEET AT THE CEMETERY. Both families. Mom and Dad, Max's parents. Grace rides on Dad's back, clutching and squeezing his neck until his face turns the shade of Mom's lipstick.

"It's by the tree. Right?" Grace asks Max as we pass our parents and head for the grassy hill and magnolia tree.

Max slides his fingers into mine, and we take the lead. We're not in a hurry, but Max's strides speed up as if he needs to get where we are going before anyone else.

Dr. Nelson and her new boyfriend, Dr. Hart, straggle behind. They're wearing matching headbands because they have the same poufy, unruly hair. I'm already picturing their kids, or at least a daughter like Merida from the movie *Brave*. Dr. Nelson is here because my mom asked her to follow us back to the house after we leave the cemetery. Mom wants Dr. Nelson there when we move out of the house. Everyone's smiling now—even Mom and Dad—but when we return home, voices will hush and mouths will straighten. It might be serious for a while, but I'm ready. I can handle it.

Dad and Mom are taking a break from each other, from their marriage, from their lives together. "Maybe temporary, maybe permanent," Mom said. "Time to figure things out," Dad said. "We'll meet for lunch after our Friday counseling sessions," Mom shared as if a promise, "and we will keep moving forward. Change isn't always permanent, you know. At least it doesn't have to be."

Mom and I are moving in with Dr. Nelson, at least for a couple of months. Grace, too, but Grace was already living there, so it's not as much of a move for her as it is for me. I won't be living next door to Max anymore. I'll be miles away, living a block from the college. Two blocks from Henry's girl-friend, Jen. She's promised to introduce me to her college friends, and I've promised to experience something new.

Our house goes on the market in a month. Paperwork has slowed the process, but for now, that's the plan. We're waiting for the final stamp telling us the lawsuit has been officially dropped. Max's dad was the first to tear up the paperwork and chuck it into the fire pit at the barn. My dad followed. They both held the papers over the pit and watched them go from orange to black to gray. I worry about our dads. I'm not sure they'll ever go back to being the best buds they once were.

Mom says she won't outstay her welcome at Dr. Nelson's, but Dr. Nelson's welcome mat looks something like this: ∞. The love she has for my mom, for Grace, and me also forms a similar shape.

The thought of leaving Max and the place I grew up in hurts. But we both believe the change will benefit everyone. Last year crushed us and left us both angry yet clinging to love. It's strange how anger and love oppose each other but sometimes work together to navigate you through the tough times.

The road to change isn't always straight, though—it's curvy and narrow and full of speed humps and bumps and bottom-out-your-car potholes. And sometimes in the middle of the journey, when everything around you is a muddled mess, the clearing at the end of the road is hard to see. Sometimes, only footsteps from your face, through broken branches and piles of leaves, there's an exit leading you out of the darkest forest and near the glassy lake. The clearing—full of sunshine and hope and bright light—might burn your eyes at first, but after they adjust, you'll see the beauty that surrounds you and the pain will subside.

"There it is," Max says, and squeezes my hand before releasing and wrapping his arm around me. I tuck my arm around Max's waist, and we guide each other toward the tree.

Mom places a bundle of purple flowers beside Kate's headstone, and as soon as she backs away, everyone moves forward to drop off their flowers, too. Max's mom and dad hold hands while his mother places a dozen roses at Cal's plot next to Kate's. Dr. Nelson tucks a bouquet of colorful daisies into the flower mount, and Dr. Hart lays his bundle of lilies to the side. Jen joins Henry as Umé steps up behind me and places her warm hand on my shoulder like she did at my sister's funeral, like she's always done. I drop my weight against her, and Umé combs my hair with her fingers.

We didn't have the money to move Kate's body next to Cal's, but since the headstone hadn't been placed or even made yet, Dr. Nelson took action. She set up a fund at the college, and Dr. Hart was the first to donate. It's how the two met. Jen helped rally friends and professors to contribute to the fund to help move Kate's casket and have her buried next to Cal. They would have wanted it that way.

OUR SONG ENDED BUT THE MELODY LIVES ON

KATE REGAN

FRANK

MAY 5, 2000—DECEMBER 30, 2018

CALVIN "CAL" THOMAS

GRANGER

JUNE 16, 2000— DECEMBER 20, 2018

Since We Last Spoke

Lyrics by Kate Frank for Cal Granger

Do they know how much I miss you?
Can they understand what I feel?
Sympathy so unreasonable
The pain all too real

When I'm alone and broken in two
Crying over the hurt from losing you
There's still so much I want to say
But I'm missing you in that way

Since we last spoke and you said we were stars
You played full of love and I sang with my heart
Best friends in this life and in the next
If I'd only known our steps

I want you to know I'm sorry
I need you to know I cared
So much has been ripped from us
And I'm swallowed by despair

Since we last spoke and you said you loved me
Did you mean it like that?
I have questions I need answered
And I'll never have you back

Since we last spoke I have much to say
I love you
Always and forever in that way

52

One year later

"I DON'T GIVE TWO FLYING fucks if you won the bet!" Umé shouts. "I am not crawling naked into a boat in the middle of winter!"

I'm in the canoe and technically not naked. Bra and underwear intact, I'm pushing myself out from the bank, my body wrapped in toilet paper, chin close to a full shiver as the breeze blows and snow speckles my back.

"When you lose a bet, you pay the piper!" Henry shouts from the shore.

Poor Jen, shaking her head at Henry's words. "Henry! You call yourself a good friend!"

"For God's sake, Aggi, please be careful!" Max yells, pulling at his hair and pointing at Umé. "You lose and make your friend take the heat?"

Umé laughs. "Aggi wanted to. Insisted, even!"

The canoe drifts from the bank, and I stand up, careful to balance my weight in the middle and not tip the boat. The last thing we need is Max tearing off his boots and hat and diving into icy water again.

It feels good to be back on the lake with my friends. Grace running up and down the shore chasing Pawtrick Swayze, giggling when he loops around her legs and sends her sliding into the snow. "Come here, you beast!" she shouts, and Pawtrick barks, his big floppy ears sweeping across patches of snow.

Max's parents invite Grace and me out on Fridays, or at least they did, when Mom and Dad met for counseling and lunches, and even though my parents only go to therapy once a month now, Grace and I still drive to the lake on weekends to spend time with our friends.

Max and I see each other almost every day. We've been sorting through our feelings, and if we don't see each other, we talk on the phone or send five million messages via text. We're both taking a year off from school, a gap year, but without pre-admittance to college. We're figuring out our lives. Filling the gap year we never intended to take from each other.

Max and Henry plan to get an apartment together. Well, Henry planned to move in with Jen five minutes after they had sex, but Max convinced him to slow things down a bit. "Like you and Aggi?" Henry mocked. I guess Max and I have taken our own sweet time, but tonight I plan to change that.

"Jesus George R. R. Martin Christ!" Umé shouts. "I don't approve of you not wearing a life jacket! Now say it before your boobs freeze and drop from your chest!"

I cup my hands around my mouth. It's as easy this time as it was the last. "I love you, Maxwell Granger! As much as you love yourself!"

Author's Note

THIS BOOK, THOUGH A WORK of fiction, was inspired by a year of grieving the loss of someone close. Research had equipped me with the many steps and stages of grief, but nothing quite prepares one for living through it.

One in five children will experience the death of someone close to them by the age of eighteen. In the United States alone, five to eight percent of children with siblings experience the impact of losing one. The grief that follows can be overwhelming.

If you, or someone you know, needs help coping with the loss of a loved one, you are not alone. Free, safe, and confidential support is available. For individuals under the age of eighteen, contact TeenLine at 1-800-TLC-TEEN, text TEEN to 839863, or visit www.teenline.org. For individuals over the age of eighteen, contact the Compassionate Friends at 1-877-969-0010 or visit www.compassionatefriends.org.

Suicide-prevention lifelines are also available for you or someone close to you. Please don't wait to seek help. The National Suicide Prevention Lifeline provides 24/7, free, and confidential support for anyone in distress. Contact the Lifeline at 1-800-273-8255 or reach them online at www.suicidepreventionlifeline.org.

Lastly, the prevalence of sibling abuse and bullying should never be ignored. According to data, sibling abuse is one of the most common forms of bullying. If you, or someone you know, is experiencing mental, physical, or sexual abuse, contact the National Child Abuse hotline at 1-800-422-4453 or www.childhelp.org/hotline.

Acknowledgments

FIRST OF ALL, THANK YOU to the many readers I've had the privilege of meeting in person and online. You are the best part of this journey.

To Melissa Edwards at Stonesong Literary Agency for her continued support and dedication to this book. She took a chance on me, and for that I am forever grateful.

Deepest gratitude to my incredible editor, Alyson Day, for your belief in this story, and for always shining a light along the twisty road of writing.

Thanks are also due to the amazing team at Harper-Teen and HarperCollins, especially Manny Blasco, Renée Cafiero, Liz Byer, Aubrey Churchward, Helen Crawford-White, and Joel Tippie. Talented artists and designers, copy editors, proofreaders, and publicists champion books with little recognition, and to them I am so grateful.

To the authors who paved the way before me and continue to offer a helping hand, a much-needed talk, or a sense of calm before a storm: Kerry Kletter, Jennifer Niven, Amy Reed, and Amber Smith.

I am also grateful to the Electric Eighteens, the Nebo Retreaters, and the amazing authors with whom I have had the honor of serving on panels. You all make this sometimes isolated profession a heck of a lot more fun. Thanks for sharing your jokes, wise words, and wine with me.

And last, thanks always to my husband and daughters. Your love and support are immeasurable, and I am honored to share this life with you.

Brenda Rufener is a technical writer turned novelist, and author of *Where I Live*—which *Bustle* named a most anticipated YA contemporary book hitting shelves in 2018. Brenda spent most of her life in the Pacific Northwest but now lives in North Carolina with her family.

www.brendarufener.com